SIPPO GHOST

The Girl
in the
Blue Tunic

Jean Ure

Hippo

For Eileen, with love

Scholastic Children's Books,
Commonwealth House, 1–19 New Oxford Street,
London WC1A 1NU, UK
a division of Scholastic Ltd
London ~ New York ~ Toronto ~ Sydney ~ Auckland

First published by Scholastic Ltd, 1997
First published in this edition, 1998

Text copyright © Jean Ure, 1997

ISBN 0 590 19795 9

All rights reserved

Printed and bound in Great Britain by
Caledonian International Book Manufacturing Ltd, Glasgow

10 9 8 7 6 5 4 3 2

Chapter One

The minute the bell rang for lights out, Hannah rolled herself into her duvet, turned her head into the pillow and began, very quietly, to weep. She had to do it quietly because of the three other girls in the dorm. If they heard her they would think she was a baby. Eleven years old and never been away from home before! Crying herself to sleep because she wanted her dad!

Thinking of Dad made the tears flow even faster. He would be on the plane now, on the way to Riyadh. Hannah had never even heard of Riyadh, before Dad broke it to her that he had to go and work there.

"It's in Saudi Arabia," he had said; but where was Saudi Arabia?

They had pulled out the old atlas and Dad had shown her.

"There! See? The top right-hand corner, just above Africa ... other side of the Red Sea."

The Red Sea! That was out of the Bible. It was miles away! Thousands and thousands! And Dad was going to be there for a whole year. Dad and Hannah had never been away from each other for longer than a night.

Hannah's tears soaked hotly into the pillow. She knew she had to be brave. She had promised Dad that she would be.

"It's a wonderful opportunity, Hanny, for both of us. Just think! When I come back we'll have enough money to buy a house of our own. Somewhere in the country, where you won't get asthma. And you're going to be at the school your mum always wanted you to go to. She'd be so happy if she knew you were there!"

And then he had hugged her and said, "Be brave! A year will soon pass."

Hannah had known that for Dad's sake she mustn't whine or grizzle or make a fuss. Dad had given up everything for Hannah after Mum had died; now it was his turn. Going to Saudi Arabia was his big chance.

"I won't be selfish and spoil it for him," vowed Hannah. "I won't! I won't!"

She had tried so very hard to be brave. She had managed to smile as he kissed her good-bye, and she had waved as brightly as she could as the taxi bore him off down the school drive, away along the curving coast road. The sea was a deep dark grey that day, crested with white as the waves came rolling shorewards. She had waved and waved until she could see him no more.

Miss Appleyard, the headmistress, had been kind to her. She had said, "You're our only new girl this term, Hannah, so I expect things will seem rather strange just at first. I'd better find someone to look after you."

She had found a girl called Charlotte Brady. Charlotte had been kind too, in an offhand way. She had shown Hannah to her dormitory and taken her down to tea and introduced her to everyone else in her class, which was Upper IIIB, and of course they had all demanded to know why Hannah was starting in the middle of the school year instead of last term along with the rest of them.

Hannah had told them, "Because my dad's got a job in Saudi Arabia and there's no one else I can stay with," and she had managed to do it without bursting into tears, even though there was a lump the size of a pigeon's egg in her throat. She had eaten her tea and eaten her supper and been as brave as brave could be and never let anyone guess that her heart was breaking. But oh, it was so difficult!

A year will soon pass, Dad had said; and of course years *did* pass. Once Hannah had been ten and now she was eleven and when Dad came home she would be twelve. But twelve was months and months away!

Hannah buried her face in the pillow, doing her best to stifle her sobs. *Dad!* she thought. She wanted her dad!

Suddenly, in the darkness, she felt an arm steal about her shoulders. She heard a voice whisper in her ear: "Don't cry! Things will get better. We all know what it's like; we've all been through it."

Hannah froze. Who was this who had come creeping through the curtain and into her cubicle?

"Soon!" whispered the voice. "It will get better, I promise!"

Hannah flipped over on to her back, but too late; whoever it was had gone. She heard a faint patter of feet across the dormitory floor, the swish of a curtain. She was too shy to peep out and see which cubicle they had gone into. But at least there was someone who understood. Someone who didn't think she was a baby. It made her feel a little bit better.

Hannah turned on to her side and snuggled her knees up to her chin, wondering which of her three dorm mates it could have been. She didn't think it was Charlotte. Charlotte came from the West Indies and had a voice that was soft and sweet like honey. It hadn't been Charlotte's voice.

And then there was Charlotte's friend, Danielle. Danielle had what Hannah's dad would call "a double-barrelled surname". Hannah had seen it printed on one of the labels on the dormitory door: Danielle Ormsby-Ashworth. Danielle was as grand as her name. Hannah couldn't imagine her understanding what it was like to feel lonely and desperate and longing for your dad. It couldn't have been Danielle.

That only left Lucy Barlow. Lucy hadn't said very much so far. She was dark-haired and small – almost as small as Hannah, who everyone said was tiny for her age. She wore spectacles and had a brace on her teeth and was serious-looking rather than pretty. It must have been Lucy.

Hannah sent her legs exploring down the bed and tucked both hands beneath the pillow. If she could just find someone to make friends with, maybe life wouldn't be quite so bad.

Next morning when she woke up she thought, Dad's in Saudi Arabia by now, and almost set herself off crying all over again. The top right-hand corner above Africa, on the other side of the Red Sea... It might as well be on another planet!

"Best be quick," said Charlotte, sticking her head through Hannah's curtains. "They get awful mad if you come down to breakfast late."

"They give you *order* marks," said Danielle.

Hannah hurried herself miserably into her clothes. The Madeley Hall uniform was a blue pleated skirt and blue sweater. Dad had said, "Mum would be so proud if she could see you! It was her dream that you should go to her old school."

Hannah sat for a long time behind a locked door in the washroom, blotting dismally at her eyes with a handkerchief. She heard Charlotte and Danielle and some of the others giggling together and splashing about in the wash-basins, then there was silence. By the time she felt strong enough to show herself, the washroom was empty.

She scrubbed at her face with her flannel and peered anxiously at her reflection in the mirror. Her reflection peered anxiously back.

I am not beautiful, thought Hannah. My mouth is too small and my teeth are sticky-out and I am *wishy washy*. Her hair was quite pretty, pale blonde and cut short with a fringe, but it had a horrid tendency to go into wisps. She looked like a rabbit, she decided. A nibbling, pink-eyed rabbit. And everybody would know she had been crying!

Hannah hurried back to the dorm only to find that all the others had gone, even Charlotte, who was supposed to be looking after her. Perhaps Charlotte thought that by now Hannah could find her own way to the dining hall. But she couldn't! Hannah had a very poor sense of direction. Dad was always teasing her about it. "Little Dolly Daydream" he called her, because she had a habit of not noticing where she was going. She would never find her way to the dining hall!

Panic-stricken, she ran down the stairs and into a long corridor with lots of doors and flights of steps at each end. Which way did she go?

"Hallo," said a voice. "Are you lost?"

It was Lucy! Hannah's heart began to bang and thump with relief.

"I thought someone had better wait for you," said Lucy. "I expect you're a bit confused at the moment, aren't you?"

Hannah nodded humbly. Lucy was so nice! It must have been her last night.

"It took me ages to find my way round," said Lucy, leading Hannah down one of the staircases. "It's because it's such an old house, all twisty and turny."

"Will we be late?" said Hannah. "Will we get order marks?"

"You won't," said Lucy, " 'cause you're new. And I won't, 'cause I waited for you."

It was Lucy who waited for her at breaktime, as well, and took her out into the playground.

"Sorry," said Charlotte. "I forgot."

"It's all right," said Lucy. "I'm looking after her now." She linked her arm through Hannah's. "Let's go and sit down and talk."

She led Hannah across the playground to a bench in the corner.

"This is my bench," said Lucy. "I often sit here."

"All by yourself?" said Hannah.

"Mostly. I like my own company. I like to read and think. I do a lot of thinking," said Lucy, shunting her spectacles up her nose with the middle finger of her right hand. "But I like talking as well, if people are intelligent. I prefer talking to rushing about playing games, don't you?"

"Well, I would actually quite *like* to rush about playing games," said Hannah, "but I'm not very often allowed."

"Why is that?" said Lucy, interested. "Do you have a weak heart?"

"No, I get asthma," said Hannah.

"Oh, brilliant! So you don't have to do boring things like netball or hockey? Oh, you are so *lucky*! I wish I got asthma," said Lucy.

"I don't think you'd like it very much," said Hannah. "It's quite frightening when you can't breathe. That's why my dad's gone to Saudi Arabia."

"What, so you can breathe?"

"So he can make lots of money, and when he comes back we're going to buy a house all of our own in the country. He thinks it will be better for me than London."

"You live in London? That's even more brilliant! I would *adore* to live in London."

Hannah thought that Lucy probably wouldn't adore living where she and Dad had lived, in a poky little flat right underneath the flyover, with no garden to play in and traffic roaring past your window day and night and all the fumes coming in and choking you.

"Why does he have to go to Saudi Arabia to make lots of money?" said Lucy.

"Well, because..." Hannah hesitated. Madeley Hall wasn't a school where poor people sent their children. Not usually. She wasn't sure that Lucy would understand if she explained that Dad had been out of work for ages and that this job was his chance of a lifetime, and that was why he had had to take it. The firm who were sending him to Saudi Arabia had agreed to pay Hannah's school fees while he was away, but only Miss Appleyard knew this.

"Can't he make lots of money in England?" said Lucy.

"Not as much," said Hannah.

"No, and grown-ups do seem to need a lot

of money, don't they?" Lucy pondered this strange fact for a few moments. "I can't say personally that it bothers me very much. I'd be quite happy on a desert island so long as there were loads of books. Which I suppose, on a desert island," she added, "there probably wouldn't be. Why were you sent to the Hovel? That's what we call it, amongst ourselves: the Hovel. Why did they choose this particular dump?"

"Oh, well, that was because my mum came here. And my mum's mum as well."

There was a pause.

"You mean your grandmother," said Lucy.

"Yes." Except that Hannah never really thought of her as her grandmother. Hannah's grandmother had been cross as hornets when Mum had got married to Dad. As a result she had never spoken to her ever again. She had never spoken to Dad or Hannah at all. It was almost like not having a grandmother.

"So why did you say there was no one you could stay with?" said Lucy. "Where's your mum? Is she divorced and married to someone who doesn't like you? Lots of people here have parents who are divorced. I have myself," said Lucy carelessly.

"My mum's dead," said Hannah.

"Oh." Lucy's face turned rather pink. "Bother!" she said. "I'm always doing that."

"Doing what?" said Hannah.

"Putting my foot in it."

"It doesn't matter," said Hannah. "It was a very long time ago. I never really knew her."

"All the same. One ought to think before one speaks," said Lucy. "What was your mum's name? When she was at the Hovel?"

"Judith Elkins."

"And what was your grandmother's name? Before she got married?"

"Dorothy Carter." Hannah had only discovered this quite recently. Her dad had told her. He had said, "You might want to try and trace some family history while you're there."

"We'll go and look during the lunch break," said Lucy. "See if they're on the boards. They've got these boards in the main hall with all the names of people who distinguished themselves. Did your mum distinguish herself?"

13

"I don't know," said Hannah.

"Mine did," said Lucy. "She got a scholarship to Oxford. She's on the boards. So's my grandmother. So will I be, probably."

Lucy said it quite matter-of-factly; she wasn't boasting.

"I am reasonably clever. And I like to work." She shunted her spectacles. "On the other hand I am positively *disastrous* at PE. I have no co-ordination, you see. I am very ungainly. People groan if I'm put on their team. Do you think you're going to like it at the Hovel?"

"I might," said Hannah, "once I've got used to it." Already she was feeling happier. Saudi Arabia was still on the other side of the Red Sea, but Lucy seemed to want to be friends and having a friend always made a difference.

"They say you can get used to anything if you try." Lucy wrinkled her nose. "The trouble with boarding school is that you can never get away from people. You're always having to *be* with them, and if you try to do things on your own they get mad and want to know why. As if it's abnormal. It's all right," said Lucy, "if you're the type. I don't personally think that I am. I need solitude. I am not gregarious. Are you?"

Hannah chewed at her thumbnail. She wasn't sure what gregarious meant.

"Do you like to *mix*?" said Lucy.

"Oh! Well – yes. Quite. But not all the time," said Hannah, hurriedly. "Just now and again. To be friendly."

"I am friendly," said Lucy. "I just don't want to live in other people's pockets."

Hannah giggled. "I suppose a pocket would be quite uncomfortable. Not much room," she said.

"Yes." Lucy frowned. "I'm afraid I haven't got very much of a sense of humour. I am basically a very serious sort of person."

Hastily, Hannah rearranged her features. "So am I," she assured Lucy.

"Well, I hope you are *quite* serious. People like Charlotte and Danny are simply frivolous. But it would be nice," said Lucy, "if you could take me out of myself. Miss Appleyard says that is what I need. She says, 'It is good to have a goal in life, Lucy, but you must learn how to relax and have fun.' Last term I was friends with Rosemary Blakemore, sort of, but she got sick of me."

"Really?" said Hannah. Fancy admitting to someone that a person had got sick of you!

"She said I was boring," said Lucy. "Do you want to try being friends with me and see if you think I'm boring?"

Hannah beamed. "Yes, please!" she said.

That lunchtime, Lucy and Hannah went into the main hall to look at the boards.

"There," said Lucy. "There's my mum. Up there. Let's see if we can find yours... Yes, look! Judith Elkins. There she is. Prefect. She was later than my mum. They'd have been in different forms. Let's look for your gran... There's mine, up near the top. Elizabeth Philpotts. Oh, and there's yours! Just above her ... Dorothy Carter. Wasn't that what you said her name was?"

"Yes." Hannah stood, head tilted, staring up at the boards. It gave her a strange feeling like goose bumps to think that the grand-mother she had never met and the mum she had hardly known might both, in their time, have stood here on this very same spot where she was standing.

"*1937–1943*," said Lucy. "They were here at the same time. My gran and yours." She linked her arm through Hannah's. "I wonder if they were ever friends, like we're going to be?"

Hannah had only a very little cry that night, hardly enough to make her pillow damp. As she fell asleep she heard Lucy's voice whis-pering words of comfort in her ear: "Things will get better, I promise you."

Things already were!

Dear Dad,

I can hardly believe it! I have been at the Hovel a whole week! The Hovel is what we call it although in fact it is extremely beautiful and interesting being an old mansion and full of history. It is very twisty and turny so that to begin with I was quite often "Dolly Daydream" and got lost! I am all right now though.

To begin with also I was a bit miserable and thought I would never settle down but then someone told me that everybody had gone through it and that things would soon get better and although I didn't believe them at the time it has turned out to be true. I would much MUCH rather be at home with you but if I have to be at a boarding school then the Hovel is the one I would choose.

Miss Appleyard the headmistress is really nice, not at all loud and barky as I had feared, and the girls are nice too, especially one that I have become friends with whose name is Lucy Barlow. She is not pretty but is very clever and comes out with these really intelligent remarks that make you stop and think. She says she doesn't care about money and would be happy to live on a desert island so long as there were books! She is going to go to Oxford when she is older as that is where her mum and grandma went.

I am doing QUITE well in class but I do not think I will ever be brilliant like Lucy. But now that I am her friend I will have to start working really hard as she does not like people who are simply frivolous!!! She is envious of me being let off games as she considers running about in the mud to be a waste of energy. I have told her that I would LIKE to run about in the mud. Do you think that next term I will be able to play tennis and rounders? It is very healthy here and I am not having any asthma. It will be lovely when you are back and we can have our house in the country. I am crossing off the days on the calendar like you said. I hope you are too.

I almost forgot to say that our class is doing a history project on "Madeley Hall in the Second World War". We all have to choose a subject, like one girl, Charlotte, who is in my dorm, is doing "The War Effort" and finding out about people knitting socks for the troops and digging for victory and another girl, Danny, is doing fashion and what people wore. I think I might do

"Everyday Life" and see how different it was from now. Like for instance I know there were steam trains and no television. It is a pity Mum's mother Dorothy Carter is not still alive or I could have asked her what it was like in those days. If she would have told me. I have found her name on one of the boards in the main hall. Lucy says surely she must have talked to me about when she was at school and I have explained that I never actually met her. Lucy cannot understand this. Nor can I, really. Why was she so cross with Mum for marrying you?

Please write back to me very quickly.

Lots of love

from

Hannah x

Chapter Two

"Now, Hannah!" Miss Maybury, the games mistress, tapped briskly with her hockey stick. "What are we to do with you, I wonder? You should at least come out and get some fresh air. Perhaps you could go for a walk round the playing field. What do you think?"

"I could stand and watch," said Hannah, hopefully. That way she would at least be able to learn the rules.

"Mmm ... well ... Yes, all right. So long as you wrap up really warmly."

Hannah put on her thick tweedy school coat and her boots and a pair of woolly gloves.

She wound a long stripy scarf round her neck and tied it in a knot.

"Excuse me for saying so," said Lucy as they trundled off together towards the playing field, Lucy shivering in her PE shorts, "but I really think you must be slightly mad. You could have stayed in school and read a book!"

"No, I couldn't," said Hannah. "Miss Maybury said I'd got to get fresh air."

"You could have told her you didn't want to get fresh air. You could have said it wasn't good for you."

"But I want to learn how to play hockey!"

"I can't imagine why." Lucy said it glumly. "It's a totally ludicrous sort of game."

"Yes, but one day I might be allowed to start playing, and it would be better," argued Hannah, "if I knew the rules."

Lucy just humped a shoulder. She really hated games where you had to run around throwing things or catching things or hitting things with sticks. "Why can't we play chess?" she grumbled.

Hannah thought that Lucy would probably be good at chess. She certainly wasn't very good at hockey; even Hannah could see that. While people like Charlotte and Danny bounded energetically up and down the field, whacking the ball as hard as ever they could, poor Lucy stood in a forlorn heap, shaking as the wind blew in from the sea, and waving her stick half-heartedly as the ball shot past.

"For goodness' sake, Lucy!" scolded Miss Maybury. "Make an effort! Keep your eye on the ball."

It wasn't Lucy's fault, thought Hannah. She was very short-sighted and was probably scared of her glasses falling off and getting trampled in the mud. Some people just weren't cut out for violent physical exercise.

Hannah wasn't sure that she was herself, but she would have liked to try. Having to stand and watch was very frustrating, and also it was cold. She was starting to shiver in spite of being muffled up in her long stripy scarf. Miss Maybury flashed past, blowing her whistle. She called over her shoulder as she ran: "Off you go, Hannah! Round the playing field! You'll get frozen stiff if you stand there much longer."

Hannah set off obediently, shoulders hunched. It was a bad habit, hunching her shoulders. She did it because of having had asthma for so long. But she hadn't been bothered by asthma for three whole weeks, and if she wanted to join in and play hockey and netball she would have to prove that she was fit. Determinedly, she held her head high and began to swing her arms like a soldier. Left, right; left, right; left—

What was that? She had seen something flitting through the trees. Hannah broke into a trot. Ahead of her, skipping in and out of the shadows, was a girl. Her hair was done in a long silvery plait which bobbed up and down as she skipped. She must have heard Hannah coming after her, because she stopped and turned. Hannah also stopped. They stood facing each other.

"Hallo!" said Hannah.

The girl said nothing. Her face was pinched, almost blue with the cold – and no wonder! thought Hannah sternly. She was dressed quite inadequately for the time of year. *No* coat, *no* scarf, *no* gloves, only a shapeless blue tunic which buttoned at the shoulders and hung in wide box pleats to her knees, and beneath it a cream-coloured blouse several sizes too large.

Everything seemed to be several sizes too large: the blouse, the tunic, the heavy lace-up shoes, the thick knee-length socks. It was because the girl herself was so tiny. Even tinier than me, marvelled Hannah, who was used to being told that "You are far too thin, child!"

This girl was skinny as an elf – thistledown light, as if a puff of wind might carry her away. The legs that protruded from beneath the blue tunic were frail as twigs, while the small head with its silvery plait drooped and dipped like a flower on a stem.

Round her waist hung a pale blue sash with fringed ends. I wish I had a sash like that, thought Hannah. She pointed.

"That's nice," she said. "I like that!"

The girl looked down at the sash, then back again at Hannah. Her eyes were round and pale, almost colourless. Still she said nothing.

"Aren't you cold?" said Hannah. "I'm cold

even in all this." She waved her gloved hands. "I'd have thought you'd be freezing."

For a moment it seemed as if the girl might be on the point of saying something, but then from the edge of the woods came the sound of Lucy's voice, calling: "Hannah! Where are you?"

Instantly, the girl turned and went flitting off. Scared of being caught, thought Hannah. She obviously ought not to have been there.

"Hannah!" Lucy appeared through the trees. "Miss Maybury sent me to find you. It's time to go in."

They walked back together across the playing field. The others had already gone.

"What were you doing?" said Lucy curiously.

"I went for a walk. Miss Maybury told me to."

"I thought I heard you talking to someone."

Hannah hesitated. She didn't want to get the strange little elfin girl into trouble.

"Were you talking to yourself? It's all right," said Lucy. "I talk to myself all the time. I have these really long conversations. Sometimes I even have arguments."

That still didn't make it normal, thought Hannah. How could you have an argument with *yourself*?

"I was talking to this girl," she said.

"What girl?"

"A girl in the woods."

"What was a girl doing in the woods?"

"I don't know. She didn't say."

"Did you ask her?"

"There wasn't time," said Hannah.

Lucy frowned, and swished with her hockey stick.

"You mean she was someone from outside?"

"I suppose so. She wasn't wearing our school uniform."

"Maybe she was one of the domestic staff."

"Mmm." Hannah admitted the possibility, though rather doubtfully.

"I mean, if she *wasn't*, then she oughtn't to have been there. This playing field is private," said Lucy. "People from outside aren't allowed in. Trespassers can be prosecuted.

What did she look like?"

"Little and thin," said Hannah.

"Sounds like Yvonne. She's little and thin. She works in the kitchen. I'll show her to you."

"All right," said Hannah.

She hoped that Lucy might forget, but Lucy's brain was needle-sharp; she never forgot things. At lunchtime, in the dining hall, she jogged Hannah's elbow and whispered. "Look, that's Yvonne ... the one putting things out. Was it her?"

Hannah took one look at Yvonne and shook her head. "No."

"Are you sure?"

"Positive." Yvonne might be little and thin but there was nothing fragile about her. She looked tough and wiry. And although you couldn't see her hair, because of it being hidden under a cap, her face was much sharper with a pointy nose and freckles. And anyway, she was too old – at least sixteen. The girl in the blue tunic had only been about Hannah's age.

"In that case," said Lucy, helping herself to

a generous portion of chips (in spite of not having any material needs, Lucy actually ate a great deal more than Hannah), "she must have come down from the estate. I expect you ought to report it, really."

"Do I have to?" said Hannah.

"Well, you don't *have* to, but she oughtn't to have been there."

"She wasn't doing any harm," pleaded Hannah. "I expect she just wanted to watch the hockey."

"Yes, but it is *private property*," said Lucy.

Hannah sighed. She liked having Lucy for a friend but there was no denying that just occasionally she could be rather grand. Hannah thought of it as "getting on her high horse". When Lucy got on her high horse she even talked differently. She talked in a way that at Hannah's old school would have been considered posh. Mrs Dukes, who took them for drama, said that Hannah had a London accent. She was making Hannah do special speech exercises to cure her of it.

Hannah hadn't realized that she had an accent. She had thought she spoke quite normally. And even if she didn't, she couldn't quite see why it was something that needed to be cured, but apparently it was. It made Mrs Dukes shudder and say things like, "*Nothing*, Hannah! Not *nuffink*." So now Hannah was having to recite *Round the rugged rocks* and *Peter Piper picked a peck of pickled peppers* every day. Dad probably wouldn't recognize her next time she spoke to him on the phone.

"Imagine," said Lucy, "if strange people from outside kept running into *your* back garden."

"We haven't got a back garden," said Hannah.

Lucy tutted, impatiently. That was the sort of remark she considered frivolous.

"If you *had*," she said.

"I'd ask them what they were doing there."

"And tell them to get out. *Wouldn't* you?"

"I suppose so," said Hannah.

"Well, then!" Lucy plonked her plate of chips on to a tray. "Where's the difference between someone walking into your back garden and someone walking on to our playing field?"

Hannah couldn't quite put her finger on it, but she felt that there was one.

"There isn't any difference at all," said Lucy. "It's trespassing and you can't deny it!"

Hannah didn't want to deny it, she just wanted to get on with her lunch. Lucy did sometimes tend to nag at a subject.

"If you see her again. . ." began Lucy.

"I don't expect I will," said Hannah.

"No, but if you do you ought to tell her."

Not having Lucy's super A1 all-powerful brain, Hannah forgot about the girl in the blue tunic. She practised *Round the rugged rocks* and *Peter Piper* and tried very hard to say "nothing" instead of "nuffink" and went on crossing days off on her calendar, though sometimes, now, she didn't always remember. Then, on Saturday morning, the Under-13 hockey team had a match against another school's Under-13 hockey team and Charlotte and Danny were playing in it.

"You are going to come and watch, I hope?" said Charlotte. "I mean, after all, we are in the same dorm."

"I never watch hockey matches." Lucy's attitude was as lofty as ever. "I consider it a total waste of time. I have some reading to catch up on."

Charlotte and Danny turned, rather aggressively, to Hannah.

"You?" they said.

"I'll come," said Hannah.

It was while she was standing there, in the drizzling rain, that she saw the girl in the blue tunic again. She was watching the hockey from the shelter of the trees. She still wasn't wearing any coat.

Heart thumping, Hannah made her way round the edge of the field. She knew she had to say something – ask the girl who she was and what she was doing. Hannah had to warn her that she was trespassing and might get into trouble.

This time the girl didn't run away when Hannah approached her. She shrank back slightly amongst the trees, but stood her ground.

"Excuse me," said Hannah, "but did you know that you're trespassing?"

The girl looked at her out of her pale eyes. Her mouth formed the word. "Trespassing?" It came out almost as a whisper.

"I'm sorry," said Hannah. "I expect you just wanted to watch the game. But this is private property. It belongs to the school."

There was a silence.

"You could get into trouble," said Hannah. She said it as gently as she could. She felt almost protective towards the girl. There was something strangely sad and waif-like about her.

"I mean," said Hannah, "if Miss Maybury saw you."

The girl's eyes slid away from Hannah and back to the hockey pitch. She watched for a few moments as the figures ran up and down.

"Is Anne Marley still captain?" she said. Her voice was a thin trail of sound. "Is she still head of games?"

"I'm afraid I don't know," said Hannah. "I only just came here this term. I don't know everyone's names yet. . . What's yours?"

"Daisy," said the girl.

Daisy. Well, at least she had discovered her name.

"I'm Hannah," said Hannah.

At that moment the Hovel scored a goal and all the spectators started to clap. Daisy's little pinched face broke into a smile. She beat her hands together ecstatically.

"Two to us and one to them!"

"They probably wouldn't mind," said Hannah, "if you asked permission. If you said, 'Please can I come and watch the hockey?' Because if you don't, you see, it's a – well, it's a criminal offence! It's like going into someone's back garden. But if you went to Miss Appleyard—"

"Who is Miss Appleyard?" said Daisy.

"She's our headmistress. She's really nice. You could go to her and you could—"

"What about Miss Ruskin?"

"Miss Ruskin?" Hannah sorted quickly through all the teachers whose names she could remember. Which one was Miss Ruskin?

"Miss Ruskin's so beautiful," said Daisy. "I adore her."

"Well, all right. If you know Miss Ruskin perhaps you could go and ask her. You—"

"Hannah!" Miss Maybury was striding towards her. There was a look of concern on her face. "Hannah, what are you doing out here in the pouring rain? Take yourself back indoors and change out of those wet clothes immediately! And you'd better get a hot drink while you're about it. I don't want to be held responsible for you going down with something."

Hannah hadn't realized that the drizzle had turned to a downpour. She was rather wet, now she came to think of it. But if she was wet, Daisy must be even wetter. Of course she had disappeared the minute she heard Miss Maybury's voice, which just went to show that she *did* know she oughtn't to be there.

But I told her, thought Hannah. I told her she was trespassing.

She went back indoors and dutifully changed out of her clothes and fetched herself a hot drink from the drinks machine in the dining hall. Hannah hated being fussed over and told to look after herself, but she knew that Dad had impressed on Miss Appleyard that "Hannah is delicate." Being delicate was such a bore! And anyway, she thought, I don't believe I am any more.

She took her drink upstairs to the junior common room, where she found Lucy with her nose buried in a book as usual.

"I saw her again," she said.

"Saw who? That girl?"

Hannah nodded. "I told her," she said proudly. "I told her she was trespassing and ought to ask permission."

"Ask permission? Why should they give her permission?"

"She likes to watch the hockey. She wanted to know if – " Hannah rumpled her brow, trying to remember – "if Anne Marley was still captain."

"No, she isn't; it's Amanda Jackson. I've never heard of anyone called Anne Marley."

"And Miss Ruskin," said Hannah. "Who's Miss Ruskin?"

"Haven't the faintest idea. Nobody *I* know."

"She says that she's beautiful and that she adores her."

"Sounds to me," said Lucy, "as if she's got a screw loose."

Hannah had to admit that the same thought had crossed her mind. Was Daisy quite all there? She did seem a trifle simple.

"But I'm sure she's harmless," she said. "She's a bit sad, really . . . all pale and thin and kind of pathetic."

"She shouldn't be there," said Lucy. "We ought to report her."

"But she was only watching," pleaded Hannah. "And now I've told her. I don't expect she'll try it again."

Lucy pressed her lips into a thin line. "On your own head be it," she said. Lucy was given to making these sort of remarks.

"What do you mean?" faltered Hannah.

"I mean," said Lucy, "if anyone starts *losing* things we shall know who to blame."

Dear Hannah,

Your letter was wonderful! I can't tell you how happy it made me to know that you have found a friend already and are settling down. I always thought that you would; you take after your mum. You have a sunny personality and you get on with people. (Unlike your grumpy old fuddy-duddy of a dad!) Lucy sounds like a good, sensible girl and I'm sure you'll get on famously together.

I too am settling down but miss you very much. Yes, I'm still crossing off the days as fast as I can go! Every time I cross one off I think about you. Let's decide what sort of house we'd like. An old one? A new one? A bungalow? A cottage? Big garden? Small garden? Tell me what you think.

You ask me why your grandmother was so cross when Mum got married to me. I think partly it was because your mum was all she had in the world and she didn't want to let her go, and partly because (I am sorry to say this) your gran was something of a snob. She came from a "good" family and I came from a very very poor one. She felt that your mum was letting the family down by marrying beneath her. I have always felt guilty about this, especially during these last couple of years when I have been out of work and couldn't give you all the things you should have, but I can only tell you that your mum and I loved each other very dearly.

There is only one person I can think of who might be able to help you find out more about your grandmother and what it was like when she was at Madeley Hall (the Hovel, indeed!). That is a woman called Helen Banfield. She was your grandmother's cousin and kept in touch with your mum after we were married – the only one of the family to do so. I haven't heard from her for a good few years now. She used to live in a house called Treetops in Steeple Fold, near Salisbury, which is in Wiltshire. I've no idea whether she is still there, or even whether she is still alive (she must be getting on a bit), but you could always try writing to her. She might quite like to hear from you as she is a single woman (or used to be) and has no children of her own, which is why, I think, she was so fond of your mum. Anyway, give it a go and see what happens.

It is excellent news that you have not had asthma! The sea air is obviously good for you. I *see no reason why you shouldn't be able to play games next term, so long as you promise not to overdo it.*

Write to me again very soon.

All my love.

Dad x

Chapter Three

At breaktime, most days, Hannah sat with Lucy on their special seat in the corner of the playground while they munched on their buns or packets of crisps and earnestly discussed the state of the world.

You had to be on your toes when you were with Lucy. She wasn't interested in idle chit-chat. What Lucy wanted to talk about was pollution and ecology and over-population. It wasn't the least bit of use trying to distract her by commenting on the beautiful new earrings that Mrs Dukes had been wearing, or pointing out, with a giggle, that Tamsin Freely was looking an absolute fright with her hair all frizzed. Lucy would just rumple her forehead and frown and go "Mmm" in impatient tones, before dragging the conversation back to the menace of the motor car or the benefits of turning vegetarian.

It was sometimes quite difficult to keep up with her, but at least, thought Hannah, my mind must be expanding. She would have lots to talk to Dad about when he came back from Saudi Arabia!

Sometimes, during the lunch break, they would wander round the grounds with Charlotte and Danny, and then the tone of the conversation would definitely be lowered. With Charlotte and Danny the talk was all of school affairs: how this person had a crush on that person, how one of the teachers was too mean for words, how somebody in the Lower Fifth had been caught smoking a cigarette and somebody else was going to be chucked out of the hockey team. Lucy huffed and puffed in superior fashion but you couldn't use your brain *all* the time, thought Hannah; you would wear it out. And anyway it was fun, occasionally, to enjoy a bit of gossip.

They were strolling round the field one lunchtime, discussing Tamsin Freely and her frizzed-up hair.

"Some people can get away with it," said Charlotte, "and some people can't."

"Yes," said Danny, "and she's one that can't."

"I wonder why she did it?" marvelled Hannah.

"No taste," said Charlotte. "She never did have."

"It's a question of aesthetics," said Lucy.

There was a pause.

"Is she speaking English?" wondered Charlotte.

"A foreign language, I *think*," said Danny.

Lucy tutted. "Your ignorance is appalling! If you would just read a book now and again—"

"Don't want to read a book."

"Well, you should!"

"Well, I don't."

The three of them walked on, arguing fiercely.

"The day of the book has *gone*."

"It's all computers now."

"Just because she's computer *illiterate*—"

Hannah let them draw ahead of her. She had just glimpsed a familiar figure in a blue tunic flitting among the laurel bushes that bordered the path. Daisy! What was she doing here, so close to school? She seemed to be trailing them.

"Han, are you coming?" Charlotte was holding open the door that led into the lower school science block.

"Yes." Hannah hurried to catch up. As she went through the door she glanced over her shoulder. Daisy was standing there, half-hidden behind a pillar. She beckoned frantically to Hannah.

"Oh, bother!" said Hannah. "I've just remembered something I forgot."

The other three continued on their way, still arguing. Hannah slipped back out and went racing over to Daisy.

"What are you doing here? What do you—"

She broke off as the sound of voices came up the path. Daisy instantly melted back into the shadows. After a moment's hesitation, Hannah squeezed in with her, between the laurels and the wall.

44

"What do you want?" she whispered.

"Did you find out about Anne Marley?"

"Yes. She isn't hockey captain any more; someone else is."

"Someone else?" Daisy's thin voice quivered in disbelief. "Who?"

"I don't know. I can't remember."

"What about Miss Ruskin?"

"Nobody's ever heard of anyone called Miss Ruskin."

"Never heard of her?"

"No." Hannah shook her head. It was dark and drippy under the laurels. Rather unpleasant. It smelt of damp earth, like fungus.

"Look," she said. "I've got to go. I've got a—"

"Never heard of Miss Ruskin?" Daisy's voice rose to a shrill piping.

"Ssh! No. And I've got a science cl—"

"What's happened to her?"

"I don't know. I told you. Nobody has ever heard of her."

Really, she began to think that Lucy was right and that Daisy wasn't quite all there. How many times did you have to repeat yourself?

"I've got to go now or I'll be late, and anyway you ought not to be here. Why aren't you at school?"

"She is so lovely," said Daisy. "I adore her!"

Hannah tutted impatiently, just as Lucy had earlier. Couldn't Daisy even respond to a simple straightforward question?

"She isn't dead, is she?" Daisy's hands reached out, imploringly, towards Hannah. "Miss Ruskin isn't dead?"

How am I supposed to know? thought Hannah.

"Please," whispered Daisy, "find out about Miss Ruskin!"

"All I can do is ask," said Hannah. "But even if I do manage to find out anything I don't see how I'm going to tell you 'cause you *ought* not to be here, and if you keep hanging around like this then sooner or later someone'll catch you and you'll get into ever such trouble. It's trespassing," she said, though even as she said it she thought that in all probability Daisy wouldn't understand the word. "This is private property."

"Look," said Daisy. Her fingers brushed

against Hannah's. It was like being touched by the wing of a butterfly. "I'll show you!"

She dipped her head and darted forward along the narrow path between the laurels and the wall. Hannah followed, somewhat doubtfully.

"See?" Daisy pointed. The wall was made out of large chunks of flint stuck together with what Hannah supposed must be cement. One of the chunks had come loose, leaving a hole about the size of a teacup.

"You can put things in it," said Daisy.

"You mean, like a letter box?"

"We can leave messages."

And if we get caught, thought Hannah, I shall get into the most enormous trouble.

"Please!" begged Daisy. "I do so want to know!"

"Well ... all right." Hannah said it grudgingly. "Just this once. But you've got to stop coming here!"

"Why?" said Daisy. "Why mayn't I come?"

"I *told* you," said Hannah. "It's *private property*." She paused to let it sink in. "Trespassers will be prosecuted!"

"Nobody ever sees me," said Daisy. She

sounded wistful. "Only you."

"Yes. Well. I ought to report you, really."

"Why?" whispered Daisy.

Heavens! How many more times did she have to tell her?

Daisy's face puckered. "I just want to know about Miss Ruskin!"

Hannah sighed. You really couldn't hold a proper conversation with someone who wasn't quite all there. At the same time you ought not to lose your temper with them. Daisy couldn't help being simple.

"I'll see what I can do," said Hannah. "I really have to go now or I shall be late."

She was late anyway, in spite of tearing up the stairs two at a time and getting herself out of breath (though not nearly as out of breath as she would have been when she was living in London, underneath the flyover).

"Well, Hannah?" Miss Porter looked at her rather coldly. Miss Porter was one of the *least* nice of the teachers. "And what have you to say for yourself?"

"Sorry," mumbled Hannah. "I forgot my books."

"Forgetfulness is no excuse. You have a timetable, have you not?" Hannah nodded. "Very well then! In future, consult it. Go and sit down."

Hannah took her place next to Lucy on the front bench.

"You *had* your books." Lucy mouthed it at her accusingly. Hannah humped a shoulder.

"I thought I'd forgotten one. I w—"

"Hannah Stevenson!" Miss Porter's eyes were like radar scanners. "Will you kindly get on with your work? You've wasted enough time as it is."

As they made their way to their private corner of the playground during afternoon break, Lucy said, "What did you really go back for?"

"I thought I saw something," said Hannah.

"Her?"

"Yes."

"And was it?" said Lucy.

There wasn't any point trying to pull the wool over Lucy's eyes. She was far too sharp. Reluctantly, Hannah said, "Yes, it was, but I've told her she mustn't come here again."

"You told her that last time!"

"I know, but she wants me to find out about this Miss Ruskin person. Then she'll stay away."

"Who *is* this Miss Ruskin?"

"I think she must have been a teacher."

"Well, she isn't now. And what's it to her, anyway?"

"Maybe she used to see her ... like when we're going to church or something."

"You mean she stands and gawps?"

"I don't think she *gawps*," said Hannah. "She's just interested."

"That is *seriously* weird," said Lucy. "What business is it of hers?"

"It's like people looking at the Queen," suggested Hannah.

"Well, she can't have looked at any Miss Ruskin 'cause there isn't one. Not as far as I'm aware."

"Who do you think would know?"

"One of the staff, perhaps, but I don't see how you're going to ask them. What would you say? 'Someone who stands and gawps wondered what had happened to her'?"

"I shall make something up," said Hannah.

Lucy studied Hannah a moment, then shook her head. "I don't know why you bother. I'd just report her and have done with it."

"You wouldn't," said Hannah, "if you saw her. She's really pathetic."

Lucy snorted. "You won't think she's so pathetic when things start going missing."

"Honestly," said Hannah, "she just likes watching us. That's all."

Hannah had once had a Victorian children's book with a picture of raggedy children standing in the snow with their noses pressed to the windows of a house where rich people lived. Inside the house the rich people were warm and snug and having fun. It was a bit like Daisy gazing at the girls of the Hovel.

"I bet she comes from the estate," said Lucy.

Hannah prickled. "So what?"

"So I bet she can't be trusted, that's what!"

If Lucy could see where she and Dad had lived, thought Hannah, she would most probably conclude that Hannah couldn't be trusted either.

"You oughtn't to make judgements," she said. "You're just being prejudiced."

Lucy's cheeks grew red. "Well, I haven't seen her," she muttered.

"Well, and I have," said Hannah.

Lucy shut up after that.

Next day, Hannah went up to Mrs Dukes after drama class. She chose Mrs Dukes because Mrs Dukes was one of the friendliest of the teachers.

"Yes, Hannah?" said Mrs Dukes. "How can I help you?"

Rather shyly Hannah said, "I wondered if you could answer a question for me."

Mrs Dukes laughed. "Try me! What's the question?"

"Can you tell me if there was ever a teacher here called Miss Ruskin?"

"Miss Ruskin? Yes! I believe there was once a Miss Ruskin. I seem to remember hearing the name. But she'd retired by the time I came here. That was about five years ago. Why did you want to know?"

"Oh, it's my history project." Hannah said

it vaguely. "I'm doing research."

That evening, after tea, she wrote a note for Daisy: *Miss Ruskin has retired*. And then she tore it up and wrote another, using capital letters this time, just in case Daisy might not be too good at reading.

It was going to be difficult finding a suitable moment to slip out and place the message in Daisy's hole-in-the-wall letter box. Lucy had been right when she complained that it was impossible to do anything by yourself at a boarding school. There was always someone clamouring for your attention or wondering where you'd got to. As a rule Hannah didn't mind, but it made it rather awkward when you wanted to do something that perhaps you ought not to be doing and you didn't want anyone to know about it.

In the end she managed to sneak away just before the bell rang for supper, but even then she bumped into Charlotte and Danny on her way back.

"What *are* you doing out there," said Danny, "all by yourself in the dark?"

"Just sniffing the night air," said Hannah.

Next morning, immediately after breakfast, she couldn't resist the temptation to take a quick peek and see if her note was still there. She raced out of the dining hall ahead of the others – "I've forgotten my handkerchief!" – and hurried down the path towards the science block. Fortunately no one else was about. She dived into the laurels and burrowed along by the wall until she came to Daisy's letter box. The note had gone! Daisy must have got up really early. She must have crept down from the estate while they were all having breakfast.

Hannah felt round carefully, just to make sure, but the only thing in the letter box was a tiny feather, fawn and brown and brilliant blue. Hannah stared at it in wonderment. She was certain it hadn't been there yesterday. It must be Daisy's way of saying thank you.

Hannah placed the feather carefully in the pocket of her skirt. It was one of the nicest presents, she thought, that she had ever had.

Back in school she found Lucy waiting for her.

"What *do* you get up to?" said Lucy. "You're becoming frightfully forgetful!"

"I know," said Hannah. "I think it's old

age." She took the feather from her pocket. "Look what I found! What is it, do you think?"

"It's a feather," said Lucy.

"I know, you idiot!" Hannah pushed at her. "What sort of feather?"

"It's a jay's feather. Where did you find it?"

"Oh ... upstairs. In the dorm. It's pretty, isn't it?"

"They're quite common," said Lucy. "We've got jays all over the place at home."

Hannah had never seen a jay. You didn't tend to get them under the flyover.

"I think it's beautiful," said Hannah. "On Saturday, when we go into town, I'm going to see if I can find a teeny little vase to put it in. Just a teeny little one, about that size." She held her finger and thumb a few centimetres apart. "Do you want to come with me?"

"I suppose I shall have to," said Lucy, "since we're not allowed out on our own. I'll tell you what we could do: we could go down the market and you could look for your vase and I could look for books."

"All right," said Hannah.

It was good having Lucy for a friend.

Dear Miss Helen Banfield,

I do hope you won't mind me writing to you. I don't know if you remember me at all but my mum was Judith Elkins who was the daughter of your cousin Dorothy which means we are related sort of though I am not quite sure how. I am sorry. My dad gave me your address and said maybe it would be all right if I wrote.

The reason I am doing so is that I am now at my mum's old school Madeley Hall as my dad is in Saudi Arabia for a year and there is nowhere else that I can go. I have been here a few weeks and am enjoying it. My mum always wanted me to come here. Anyway we have been told that we are to do a history project about the last war and what it was like in those days and especially at the Hovel, which is what we call the school amongst ourselves.

I know that my gran was at the school at that time though I never met her and unfortunately she is no longer alive for me to ask. I was wondering, if you are not too busy, if perhaps you might have photos of her or letters or anything that might help in my project as what I am doing it about is "Everyday Life".

I am very sorry if I am putting you out and I will quite understand if you do not wish to write back. But anything you could tell me I will be most grateful for.

Yours sincerely,

Hannah

Chapter Four

"**W**hat I want," said Hannah, "is a really teeny *tiny* little one."

"A doll's house one." Lucy nodded. It was Saturday morning and she and Hannah were on their way to the market to look for Hannah's vase.

"I'd really like a blue one," said Hannah, "to go with the feather."

"Mmm." Lucy didn't honestly see the attraction of a feather but she was too polite to say so. You had to allow people their odd little quirks. "What are you doing at half term?" she said. "Are you going to fly out and see your dad?"

"I wish I was," said Hannah. Dad had said it was too far and too expensive. They needed to save every penny they could.

"Relatives?" said Lucy.

"Haven't got any."

"None at *all*?"

"Not on my dad's side. My dad was an orphan."

"What about your mum's side?"

Hannah crinkled her nose. "I don't know any of them. They all stopped speaking after Mum married Dad."

"*Weird!*" said Lucy.

They walked for a bit in silence.

"So what are you going to do?" said Lucy.

Hannah heaved a sigh. "I'm supposed to be going back to London to stay with our neighbour that lived next door."

"Don't you want to?"

"No, I don't," said Hannah. Mrs Rumbold herself wasn't so bad, apart from being rather big and noisy, but she had two horrible great lumping sons who teased Hannah and bullied her and made her life a misery. Truth to tell, she was rather dreading it. She looked hopefully at Lucy.

"What about you?"

"Me?" said Lucy. She kicked with her foot at the bottom of someone's fence as they passed. "I'm staying at school."

"Oh! Maybe I could do that as well," said Hannah. It wasn't as exciting as being invited back to Lucy's place would have been, but it was heaps better than going to Mrs Rumbold's. "It might be quite fun if we were together."

"You don't have to stay just because of me," said Lucy. "I don't need people taking pity on me. I can fend for myself, I can!"

Hannah looked at her rather doubtfully. "Why can't you go home? Is your mum away?"

"No, she's too busy working and having fun with her new boyfriend. She doesn't want me around. Which is all right by *me*," said Lucy. "I'd just as soon stay here. She needn't think I care! I'll stay here all year round if that's what she wants."

She kicked again, rather more fiercely this time. "It's the only reason she sent me to boarding school in the first place – just to be rid of me."

Hannah stared at her, shocked. "I thought she sent you here 'cause it was where she came."

"Yes, and she hated it. But she says it gets me off her back." Lucy jutted her chin, but not before Hannah had seen a tear go rolling down her nose. "Needn't think *I* care," she muttered.

Hannah felt awkward, and a bit helpless. Lucy wasn't a person you expected to cry.

"Haven't you got any aunts and uncles?" she said. In Hannah's experience, everyone except herself automatically had aunts and uncles.

Lucy dashed at her eyes. "Why should they have to put up with me just because *she* doesn't want to? Not anything to do with them, am I? They've got their own lives to lead."

"I'm sure she does want you *really*," said Hannah.

Lucy whirled round on her. "What do you know about it?"

"N-nothing," stammered Hannah. But surely people's mums always wanted them? Hannah's dad wanted Hannah. The only reason he had gone to Saudi Arabia was to make enough money to buy a house for them to live in together. Poor Lucy! No wonder she was a bit prickly at times. In future Hannah would make allowances for her. She would remember that Lucy's mum just wanted to be rid of her.

"Next time Dad rings I'm going to tell him that I don't want to go to Mrs Rumbold's," she said. "I'm going to tell him that I want to stay on at school."

"You don't have to stay just to keep me company," muttered Lucy.

"I won't be," said Hannah. "I'll be staying 'cause I don't want to go to Mrs Rumbold's."

"Why don't you? What's wrong with her?"

"She's got these boys," said Hannah. "Jody and Kevin – they're horrible!"

"Boys always are," said Lucy.

They walked on towards the market, telling each other tales of all the boys they had known who were horrible.

Hannah had known more than Lucy because Hannah had been at a school where there were some. Lucy really hadn't had all that much experience. Even her primary school had been all girls. It was good, for once, to be able to feel just a little bit superior.

Down in the market they grubbed happily through the book stalls, the junk stalls, the "Under £10 genuine antique stall". Lucy came away with an armful of paperbacks, Hannah with her teeny tiny little vase. It was patterned in mysterious swirls of blue and gold and was every bit as teeny and tiny as she had hoped – hardly any bigger than her thumb.

"What I'm going to do," she said as they walked back through the school gates, "I'm going to see if I can find some more feathers and make a bunch of them."

"There's feathers all over the place," said Lucy. She already had her head buried in one of her new books. She couldn't wait to get back and start reading.

"Yes, but they've got to be pretty ones," said Hannah. "I don't want just—" Hannah broke off. Her eyes widened accusingly. Daisy was standing there, bold as brass, in the middle of a flower-bed, watching them – "just ordinary ones," mumbled Hannah. "Only . . ." her gaze slid back to Daisy. "Only ones that are—"

"Pretty," said Lucy. She looked up. "What's the matter? What are you gawping at?"

"I – thought I saw a feather," said Hannah. "Oh! Look! There's Charlotte and Danny!"

She pointed ahead, hoping to divert Lucy's attention, but fortunately Lucy hadn't seen anything. Lucy quite often walked past people without seeing them. Partly it was because she was so short-sighted, and partly it was because she had a habit of trying to walk and read at the same time. She had been known to bump into lampposts before now.

Hannah risked a quick glance over her shoulder. That wretched Daisy! She mouthed at her, "*Go away!*" The eager smile that had been on Daisy's lips quivered and drooped. Forlornly, she turned and began to trail off across the flower-bed. Now Hannah felt mean. She felt as mean as she had on the day she had smacked Mrs Rumbold's cat for stretching out a paw and pulling a thread in Hannah's new cardigan. The cat had only been trying to be friendly. So had Daisy. But she had told her! She had *told* her she ought not to trespass. And fancy walking across a flower-bed! However simple she was, she ought to know better than that. It really is too bad, thought Hannah.

She decided to forget about Daisy. Sooner or later a member of staff was bound to catch her. Then perhaps she would wish that she had listened.

Hannah took her beautiful blue-and-gold vase up to the dorm and stuck her feather in it. Then she tore a sheet of paper off the special airmail note pad that Dad had given her for sending letters to Saudi Arabia and angrily, in big capital letters, wrote: IF YOU DO NOT STOP COMING HERE YOU WILL GET INTO TROUBLE.

There would be just time to slip out and post it in the hole-in-the-wall letter box before the bell rang for lunch. She didn't know whether Daisy ever looked in there during her wanderings about the school grounds, but at least Hannah would feel she had done all she reasonably could. Perhaps Daisy might take more notice of something that was written down.

Hannah stole out of school by a side door and raced round the path towards the science block. She ducked down beneath the laurels, crept along by the wall and stuck her hand into the letter box. Something was in there! She groped at it. It felt like another feather. *Two* feathers! She couldn't see them properly under the laurels. There wasn't enough light.

Hannah emerged, backwards, on to the path. Two tiny feathers, one brown-and-white and stripy, the other a brilliant yellowy-green. Who could have put them there? Only Daisy!

She stood a moment, undecided. It had been kind of Daisy to find the other feathers for her. The note that Hannah had written, on the other hand, was rather cross. It certainly wasn't at all friendly. Slowly she scrunched it up and stuffed it into her pocket. Maybe the feathers were Daisy's way of saying sorry and that she wouldn't trespass any more. I shall trust her, thought Hannah. I shall trust her and see what happens.

After lunch, she went back up to the dorm and arranged the two new feathers in her vase. They were every bit as pretty as flowers, in Hannah's opinion. Better than flowers, really. Flowers that had been cut were sad because you knew that they were dying. Feathers wouldn't die. They will still be here, thought Hannah, when Dad gets back from Saudi Arabia.

On Sunday, Dad telephoned her. He did it once a week, just to say hallo. They never spoke for long because of the cost and Dad having to save money for the house they were going to buy, but it was long enough for Hannah to ask if she could stay on at school instead of going to Mrs Rumbold's.

"Well, if you really want to," said Dad.

"I do," said Hannah, " 'cause Lucy's going to be here. And I really hate the thought of going to Mrs Rumbold's."

"In that case," said Dad, "you have my permission. You'd better speak to Miss Appleyard and let Mrs Rumbold know."

Hannah flew back to join the others in the junior common room.

"I'm staying!" she said. "We can be together over half term!"

Lucy didn't jump up and down and hug her or cry "Brilliant!" or "Ace!" as Charlotte and Danny would have done. Showing emotions was not Lucy's way. But she took off her spectacles and began to polish them rather vigorously with a clean part of her handkerchief and very calmly said, "Good. We'll have the place to ourselves and be able to get lots of talking done," so Hannah knew that she was pleased.

During the week, after a lot of careful thought, Hannah wrote another note to Daisy and posted it in their letter box. This one said, DEAR DAISY, THANK YOU VERY MUCH FOR THE FEATHERS. THEY ARE LOVELY. BUT I AM WORRIED IN CASE YOU GET INTO TROUBLE

BEING HERE. YOUR FRIEND HANNAH.

Friday was the day before half term. While everyone else was packing their cases and Lucy was deep in one of her new books, Hannah stole away beneath the laurels and discovered that the note had been taken and yet another feather left in its place. Pure white, this time. Like a swan's, thought Hannah, though probably it was just a sea-gull's. She went skipping back up to the dorm with it, to add to the others. Four was almost getting to be a bunch!

Charlotte and Daisy had finished their packing and the dorm was empty. Hannah arranged her new feather and turned to go back downstairs but stopped as Lucy suddenly appeared in the doorway.

"Well!" said Lucy. She looked feverish and excited. Her eyes were glittery behind their spectacles. "Now you've gone and done it! It's happened! I told you it would!"

"What's happened?" said Hannah. There had been an odd note of triumph in Lucy's voice.

"Katy Eckhart's had some money stolen!"

Flat slappy goose feet went marching down Hannah's spine.

"S–so?" she stammered.

"So I bet we both know who pinched it! That girl that keeps hanging around – that one I told you to report and you wouldn't!"

"Why should it be her?" said Hannah.

" 'Cause Katy was out on the field and she took off her blazer and hung it over a branch and when she went to get it she discovered her money had gone . . . a whole ten-pound note," said Lucy. "*Now* perhaps you'll go to Miss Appleyard!"

"I don't see why I should," muttered Hannah. Katy Eckhart shouldn't have been carrying a ten-pound note round with her in the first place, specially not in her blazer pocket. It was asking for trouble.

"I'll tell you why you should," said Lucy. "Because it's your fault for not doing it in the first place! If you'd gone to Miss Appleyard when I said, Katy wouldn't have had her money pinched."

"How do you know?" said Hannah. "You

haven't any proof!"

"It's the law of probabilities," said Lucy.

"You can't go telling tales on someone just because of the law of probabilities! It could get her into trouble all for nothing."

"I don't call trespassing on other people's property *nothing*. And they're always stealing, those people up on the estate. The police are there practically every week. Half of them," said Lucy, "have been in *prison*."

Hannah refused to be impressed. "We don't even know that she comes from the estate."

"Where else could she come from? There isn't anywhere else near."

"Well, maybe not, but just because people don't live in rich houses," objected Hannah, thinking of the flat beneath the flyover, "doesn't mean they're thieves."

Lucy narrowed her eyes.

"You mean you're just going to stand by while Katy has ten pounds taken and not do anything about it?"

"Katy can afford to have ten pounds taken." She was always going round boasting about how much money her dad earned. All they ever heard was "my new pony", "our new swimming pool", "Dad's new car". Even Danny, whose parents were *seriously* rich, didn't carry on like that.

"She was breaking the rules, anyway," said Hannah.

"That's not the point. The point *is*, there's a thief on the premises. And if you don't go to Miss Appleyard," said Lucy, "you'll be an accessory."

Hannah said nothing. She wasn't going to lower herself by asking what an accessory was.

"*Well?*" demanded Lucy. "Are you going to or not?"

Hannah thought of the feathers and the eager smile that had quivered and drooped.

"I can't," she said. "Not without proof." It wouldn't be fair.

"I see." Lucy shunted her spectacles. "In that case—"

"If we hadn't been friends," burst out Hannah, "you wouldn't ever have known about her!"

Lucy regarded Hannah pityingly.

"I really fail to understand," she said, in what Hannah privately thought of as her "squashing" voice, "how that has any relevance."

"It was confidential! If you go and tell," said Hannah, "it will be a – a betrayal of friendship!"

There was a pause.

"Maybe I won't tell *this* time," said Lucy, "but if it happens again I shall feel duty bound."

Hannah struggled very hard to make allowances and to think of Lucy's rotten mother who sent her away to boarding school just to be rid of her, but the words came shooting out before she could stop them.

"Why do you always have to be so pompous?"

Lucy tossed her head. "I'd rather be pompous than friends with a *thief*!"

My dearest Hannah,

How very lovely to hear from you! Like you I am not quite sure how we are related – some kind of cousins twice removed, perhaps? – but related we certainly are.

It is a great shame that you never met your grandmother. The fault was entirely hers. Fond though I was of my cousin Dorothy, I fear that she could be very "stiff-necked" and full of family pride. But from the way you write I feel sure she would have enjoyed having you as a granddaughter. Such a pity!

Regarding your history project, I have some old photograph albums and various "bits and pieces" somewhere down in the cellar. As soon as I am able, I will look them out for you. You will have to forgive me not doing it straight away but I am not as young as I was and suffer rather badly from my knees! They creak and groan and are not very good at getting me up and down the cellar steps. But I will do it, I promise.

I am trying to think what life would have been like at Madeley Hall during the war. I went to a day school myself but I expect that life at a boarding school would not have been so very different. We had ration books, of course, for food, and "coupons" for clothing, but they did not concern us children very much.

What else can I think of? Oh, yes! Something rather dreadful called "Cod Liver Oil of Malt" springs to mind. It came in a jar and was a disgusting dark brown colour, very thick and gluggy. We had to take a spoonful of it every morning as it was thought to be good for us. Some people enjoyed it but I'm afraid with me it was a daily battle. I hated it! On the other hand I rather liked the dried eggs — bright yellow powder that you mixed with water and then cooked — and also the concentrated orange juice that was given to us as children.

There wasn't much butter, as I recall, and quite often we had to eat bread and marge. I remember that on one occasion my parents had taken in some refugee children from London and my mother gave them butter as a treat and it made them sick! They had never tasted it before. Today that would not be so unusual, would it? Lots of people never eat butter. Margarine is considered healthier for you.

I am trying to think back and remember about

clothes. We had to wear some rather appalling garments called "liberty bodices" to protect our chests from the cold, and "Chilprufe" vests underneath them. Then there were thick ribbed stockings for the older girls and long woollen socks for the younger ones, held up by elastic garters. We were well and truly muffled up in those days! But you have to remember that it was not so very long since Victorian times.

For games we had "Aertex" shirts and divided skirts which I think today would be called culottes. Lace-up shoes; no slip-ons. And in the summer we had Clark's sandals, very plain and wholesome and made to last. No jeans or even trousers, though some of the women had started to wear "slacks". My mother never did. She thought it was not quite nice. She also frowned upon women who went to work with their hair in curlers and their heads tied up in scarves, but you see there were no perms in those days, which is why most of us girls whose hair was not naturally curly wore it "bobbed" with a fringe, or else with a ribbon or hair slides to hold it back.

Oh, dear! What a lot of memories. I hope some of it has been helpful but you must ask me if there *is anything special that you want to know.*

One thing perhaps you might not be aware of and that is that your grandmother had a younger sister, Margaret, who was also at the school. Between you and me, she was my favourite of the two. Dorothy could be a tiny bit snooty, but Margaret was a sweet little soul. Unfortunately she never survived the war. Only one bomb was ever dropped on Madeley Hall and poor little Margaret just happened to be in the wrong place at the wrong time. She was three days short of her twelfth birthday. It was especially tragic because my brother Kenneth had been going to visit her and take her out for the day as a birthday treat. She was so looking forward to it! Margaret was madly in love with Kenneth. All the girls were – he was very good-looking! – but to little Meg he was like a god. She worshipped him.

Well, I must close now and get some lunch for my poor starving pussy who weighs at least a ton and last had a nibble at something as long ago as half an hour. His name is Panufnik. Fat Cat Panufnik. (Pan for short.) Maybe I shall be able to introduce you to him one day. It would be wonderful if we could meet and get to know each other. What are you doing for the Easter holiday? If you have nowhere else to go, you could always come and stay with me and Pan and even bring a friend if you wanted. We could do with some young faces around the place.

> Very best wishes
>   from your
>   cousinly relative,

Helen

PS If you write back — as I hope you will — perhaps you should call me Cousin Helen? So much more friendly than Miss!

Chapter Five

It was the first day of half term and all the school had packed up and gone, save for a small handful of girls and staff. Hannah was mooching disconsolately round the field, hands dug deep into the pockets of her coat, shoes scuffing at clumps of grass.

It was all supposed to have been such fun! She and Lucy together, doing their own thing – talking, reading, going into town. Instead Lucy was shut away by herself, nose in a book, refusing to answer when Hannah spoke to her, while Hannah wandered the field and scuffed at grass. She and Lucy hadn't quarrelled exactly, but Lucy was making it plain that she didn't want to talk. It seemed that Hannah was no longer regarded as worthy. A person who could make friends with a thief...

But I don't believe that Daisy *is* a thief! thought Hannah. It was true she had no real reason for thinking so, but then Lucy had no reason for thinking that she was. Just because she came from the estate! Hannah blinked back angry tears. That was snobbery. It was *prejudice*!

In the meantime, how was she going to keep herself amused for the rest of the week if Lucy went on sulking? You couldn't read all the time, and the only other pupils who had stayed at school were sixth-formers. She supposed, if she were to ask them very nicely, one of them might agree to take her into town, but who wanted to go into town with a sixth-former? She wouldn't know what to talk about and they would think she was just a babyish nuisance. She was almost beginning to wish that she had gone to Mrs Rumbold after all. At least if she had gone to Mrs Rumbold she would have been free to go out on her own and even catch a tube train if she felt like it, and travel to places. This was like being in a prison.

How horrid of Lucy to say that all the people on the estate were thieves! Perhaps rich people always said that sort of thing about poor people. They didn't understand what it was like not to have any money. But she was disappointed in Lucy. She had hoped that she was different.

Oh, and that morning she had had such a lovely letter from Cousin Helen! All about dried eggs and liberty bodices and what it had been like in the war. She could have shown it to Lucy and they could have talked about it and made notes for their projects. Cousin Helen had been really friendly. She had even invited Hannah to stay with her in the holidays and said that Hannah could bring a friend if she wanted. Now Lucy had gone and ruined it all. You could hardly take along a friend who refused to talk to you.

If anything else were stolen Lucy would go marching straight to Miss Appleyard and Hannah would be in trouble. Probably no one would ever talk to her again, and Miss

Appleyard would think, that is what comes of allowing a child who lived under the flyover to come to the school.

What was it Lucy had said that Hannah would be? An accessory. A *criminal*. Maybe she ought to have reported Daisy, thought Hannah miserably. It was sometimes very difficult to know what to do.

Hannah had reached the southernmost boundary of the playing field. There was a gate there, leading out into a lane. The senior girls were allowed to go through it, but not the younger ones unless they were accompanied. Someone was sitting on the gate, swinging her legs. It was Daisy.

"Hallo!" said Hannah.

What could you do? You couldn't ignore a person. And at least this time she wasn't trespassing. You couldn't call it trespassing, just sitting on a gate. Or could you?

"Did you get my note?" said Hannah.

By way of reply, Daisy held out her hand. A feather floated slowly earthwards. Hannah swooped on it.

"Oh! That's beautiful!" The feather was

crimson with a black tip. "Thank you very much," said Hannah. "I'm making a collection, you know. I've got five now."

And all of them given to her by Daisy. Carelessly, twirling her new feather between finger and thumb, she said, "A girl had some money stolen yesterday. She was over here on the field and she took off her blazer and hung it on a branch, and when she went to get it she found that her money had gone."

She forced herself to look at Daisy as she said it. Daisy's pale face remained as pale as ever. No tell-tale blush, not even a hint of pinkness.

"I had some money stolen once," she said.

"Really?" said Hannah. "Did you ever find who took it?"

"I know who took it. It was Georgina Redmay."

"What happened? Did you report her?"

"No." A puzzled frown rippled across Daisy's smooth brow. "I was going to, I think. Then something happened."

"So didn't she ever get found out?"

"I don't know." Daisy swung her legs. "It

was a long time ago. I can't remember. Did you find out who's captain of hockey?"

"Yes. It's someone called Amanda Jackson."

"Amanda Jackson?" Daisy sounded almost indignant. "I've never heard of anyone called Amanda Jackson!"

"Well, no one had ever heard of whoever it was that you said."

"Anne Marley. *She* was captain of hockey."

"When?" said Hannah.

Daisy put a finger to her mouth. "I can't remember..." Her voice trailed off. "What about Miss Ruskin?"

"I told you," said Hannah. Daisy had a terribly short memory. "She's retired."

"When did she retire?"

"Ages ago! About ... five years ago. How old were you five years ago?"

Daisy said nothing. Didn't she even know how old she was?

"You must have been about *six*," said Hannah. "Did you used to see her when she walked people to church?"

"She had a pink suit," whispered Daisy.

"And she smelt of flowers ... she was beautiful!"

Daisy had obviously, Hannah thought, had a great passion for Miss Ruskin. She must have stood every Sunday and watched her go by in her pink suit, smelling of flowers. Hannah remembered that when she had been six she had had a passion for a lady in the greengrocer's. She had thought her "the most prettiest lady in the whole wide world" and asked her dad why he didn't marry her. It made her blush now, as she looked back on it. So she didn't laugh at Daisy but instead, very solemnly, said, "I expect you missed her when you didn't see her any more." Hannah had missed the lady in the greengrocer's when she had gone to work somewhere else. But it didn't do to dwell.

She tried to think of some different subject to talk about.

"Where do you go to school?" she said. "I love that uniform! Specially the sash thing."

Daisy looked down at it. It was blue, with fringes. "That's Windsor, that is."

There was a pause. What's she talking

about? wondered Hannah. It occurred to her that you really couldn't attach very much importance to anything that Daisy said; she definitely wasn't quite all there. But at least she was company of a sort.

Hannah hoisted herself up on to the gate.

"We're doing a history project," she said. "All about the Hovel and what it was like in the war."

"War?" said Daisy.

"Yes, you know . . . the last war. And when I say Hovel," said Hannah, "I really mean Madeley Hall. We call it the Hovel. It's a sort of joke."

She waited for Daisy to laugh, or at least smile, but all Daisy said was, "When was it? The war?"

Hannah was shocked. Such ignorance! "1939–1945." She wasn't very good at dates as a rule, but she had had to learn these for her project.

"Was that a very long time ago?" said Daisy.

Hannah reminded herself that Daisy couldn't help being ignorant.

"A *very* long time ago. Long before you were born. Even before your mum was born." That was assuming that Daisy had a mum. If she had, thought Hannah, she certainly didn't look after her very well. Lucy would say that that was because she came from the estate. But fancy letting a child run about in the middle of February without a coat!

"My mum," said Hannah, settling herself more comfortably on top of the gate, "used to come to this school. So did her mum. I'm finding out all about it for this project that we're doing. I've written to this person that I call Cousin Helen, though she's not really. She was my mum's *mum's* cousin. So I don't know what relation that makes her and me and nor does she, but she's written back to me. Would you like me to read you her letter?"

Daisy nodded eagerly.

"All right," said Hannah. She took it out of her coat pocket and removed the letter from its envelope. "That's where she lives, see? Near Salisbury in Wiltshire. And that's her name, Helen Banfield. I called her Miss the first time I wrote to her, but she says to call her Cousin Helen 'cause it's more friendly. I think that's really nice, don't you? 'Cause she must be quite old by now."

"How old?" whispered Daisy.

"About sixty-five," said Hannah.

"Sixty-five?" Daisy stared at her.

"I worked it out," said Hannah. "She has to be. Do you want me to tell you what she says?"

Daisy swallowed.

"Do you?" said Hannah. "Or don't you?"

Slowly, Daisy nodded. Her eyes were riveted to the page. But she wouldn't be able to read it for herself, thought Hannah. She bet Daisy had a reading age of about four.

"Right." Hannah cleared her throat. "This is what she says. *My dear Hannah*—"

Reading Cousin Helen's letter to Daisy wasn't anywhere near as much fun as reading it to Lucy would have been, but Daisy was here and Lucy wasn't. Lucy was sitting sulking with her nose in a book.

"...*Very best wishes from your cousinly relative*. And then she says about calling her Cousin Helen." Hannah folded the letter, carefully, and put it back in its envelope. "It's interesting, isn't it? All that stuff about liberty bodices and cod liver oil ... ugh! It sounds disgusting. I'd have been sick! Wouldn't you?" She turned, to look at Daisy. "Cod liver *oil*? Yuck!"

Hannah leaned forward and made being-sick noises. Daisy watched her. When Hannah sat up she said, "Read again about Margaret."

"Margaret?" Hannah took the letter back out of its envelope. "Which bit?"

"Where she says about ... what happened."

"*Dorothy could be a bit snooty* – Dorothy was my gran – *but Margaret was a sweet little soul. Unfortunately she never survived the war. Only one bomb was ever dropped on Madeley Hall and poor little Margaret just happened to be in the wrong place at the wrong time. She was three days short of her twelfth birthday*," read Hannah.

Daisy's eyes bored into her. "Does that mean—"

"It means she wasn't quite twelve."

"Does it mean she was – killed?"

"Yes. A bomb fell on her. It's the sort of thing that happens in wartime. I've been reading about it. People were killed all over the place. In London they had a thing called the Blitz, and doodlebugs. And there were fires and houses collapsing and bodies being dug out of the rubble."

"Is that what happened to Margaret?"

Daisy's face had grown paler than ever. It was so pale it was almost transparent. Perhaps I shouldn't have told her about the bombs, thought Hannah. Sometimes people who were a bit simple could be extra-specially sensitive. A girl at her old school had been like that. She had often started crying for absolutely no reason at all, or not any reason that people could see.

"I'm not *exactly* sure what happened to Margaret," she said, "but I expect it was quite quick. I expect the bomb just fell on her, bang! and that was all she knew. So she wouldn't have suffered."

"But she's – been dead – all this time?"

"Well . . . yes," said Hannah.

"And her sister? And her mum and dad?"

"Her sister didn't die in the war," said Hannah. "She only died a few years ago. I don't know about her mum and dad. But I think they must be dead, 'cause if they were alive they'd be my great-grandparents and I'd know about them. See, Dorothy was my grandmother," she said, in case Daisy hadn't yet grasped the fact.

"Dorothy could be snooty," said Daisy. She said it in a small, sing-song, far-away voice.

"Yes, that's why she hated it when my mum got married to my dad. She never talked to us after that. I never even knew her."

"And K-K-K—"

"Kenneth? The one that Margaret was in love with? That's Cousin Helen's brother. I don't know," said Hannah. "I don't know what happened to him. I'll ask her. Maybe if he's alive I could write to him as well." She liked the thought of suddenly finding some family. "Though of course," she said, regretfully, "he won't be good-looking any more. He'll be an old man by now." She suddenly giggled. "He's probably tubby and bald with a big fat tum. If Margaret could look down and see him, she'd have a real shock!"

"But – she is old – too?" said Daisy.

"She would be, if she were still alive. She'd be..." Hannah wrestled with dates and figures. Mental arithmetic had never been her strong point. "She'd be getting on," said Hannah.

"How old would she be?"

Hannah looked again at the letter. "It doesn't say when it happened. But I suppose about ... sixty?" she said.

Daisy looked stunned. "As old as that?"

"Sixty isn't *that* old," said Hannah. Daisy was really being very ageist. "Mrs Rumbold's grandmother is ninety-three."

Daisy didn't seem interested in Mrs Rumbold's grandmother being ninety-three, though in fact ninety-three was an extremely interesting sort of age, in Hannah's opinion. Just think of all the things you would be able to remember! Not just the war, but even before the war. Almost as far back as Victorian times! You'd be like a living history book.

"One day," said Hannah, "we might be

sixty ourselves." And then they could look back and remember when they had only been twelve.

She slipped off the gate and put her letter back in her pocket. "I have to go now and get some lunch. I'll write to Cousin Helen and try to find out a bit more. I'll ask her about Kenneth. I'll put a note in the letter box, shall I? Because I have discovered," said Hannah, "that if you stay on the *other* side of the wall, where you're not trespassing, you can get at it just as easily. So that's what I'll do and then you won't get into trouble."

On her way back into school she was met by Lucy.

"Oh, there you are!" said Lucy. "I've been looking everywhere for you." She said it almost querulously. "Where have you been?"

"For a walk."

"By yourself?"

"Well, who else is there?" said Hannah. She wasn't going to tell Lucy about Daisy. "What did you want me for?"

"I just wanted to tell you –" Lucy said it cosily – "that it's all right, Katy didn't have her money stolen. She rang up a few minutes ago. Miss Appleyard just told me. She hadn't left it in her blazer at all!" Lucy gave a little embarrassed titter. "The stupid girl! She found it in her purse when she was unpacking. Honestly! All that fuss," said Lucy. "It just shows how mistakes can be made."

"It does," said Hannah, "doesn't it?"

"Yes. Well." Lucy shunted her spectacles. "I still think you *ought* to have gone to Miss Appleyard about that girl, but I'm sorry I thought she might have taken Katy's money just because she came from the estate. And I'm sorry I said about you being friends with a thief. I don't expect," said Lucy, humbly, "that you'll want to talk to me any more. I wouldn't, probably, if someone had said that to me."

"Oh, I don't know," said Hannah. "I think it's important, if a person says they're sorry, that one should be big enough to – to *forgive and forget*. And anyway –" she pulled out her letter – "I've got something to show you!"

She had read the letter to Daisy because there hadn't been anyone else, but it was Lucy she had really wanted to read it to. Lucy was a highly satisfactory listener. She didn't interrupt, but now and again she would nod or make quick little comments – "Dried eggs. I've read about them." "Cod liver oil? Ugh! Revolting!" – to show that she was interested and taking it all in.

"Will you go and stay?" she said, at the end.

"If Dad says I can, which I expect he will. I don't suppose –" Hannah hesitated, suddenly shy – "I don't suppose you'd like to come with me?"

"I should *love* to come with you!" said Lucy. She beamed at Hannah and slipped her arm through hers as they went down together to the dining hall. "You know what we ought to do?" she said. "We ought to find out more about that girl that was killed, because that is really *poignant*."

"Really what?" said Hannah, pretending she hadn't quite heard.

"Well – sad," said Lucy. "It is just so *sad*. I mean, when you think about it ... just one bomb falling and it had to go and kill her."

"I know. It's tragic."

"So I think we ought to find out all we can and make her the centre of our project."

"*Our* project?" said Hannah. "You want us to do one together?"

"We could. Miss Allan said we could work in pairs if we wanted."

"Yes, but—" It had never occurred to Hannah that Lucy with her superior brain would choose to work with a partner, and especially not with Hannah, who was merely average.

"Would you rather not?" said Lucy. "You don't have to. She's your discovery. You can keep her to yourself if you'd prefer."

"No, I don't mind sharing." Hannah said it quickly, before Lucy could change her mind. "I'll write to Cousin Helen and see what else she knows."

"Yes, and I'll go to the library and ask if we can look through all the old school magazines. We might be able to find her name," said Lucy.

It was good to be friends again.

Dear Cousin Helen,

Thank you very much for writing to me. Your letter was very interesting and helpful. My friend Lucy and I have decided to do our project on Margaret as we think it is very sad and poygnent (I am not sure how to spell this word) that the bomb should have fallen and killed only her. We are wondering if you could tell us any more about it, when it happened for instance. Also if you have any photographs it would be wonderful though of course I understand about your knees.

It was very kind of you to ask me to stay with you in the holidays and to meet your cat which would be brilliant as I have nowhere else to go, only to Mrs Rumbold which I have been dreading as she has two boys who I don't like and the only good thing is her cat called Ginger. I was supposed to be going to her for half term but instead stayed on at school to be with my friend Lucy who was unable to go home unfortunately for her as her mum thinks it is nice to have her out of the way.

You said that if I liked I could bring a friend with me and I would very much like to bring my friend Lucy if that would be all right. She is extremely clever and sensible and likes to talk about serious things such as over-population and the state of the world. She is my BEST friend and we sleep together in the same dorm. There are also two other girls called Charlotte and Danny but they are best friends with each other. They play a lot of hockey which Lucy doesn't like as she is short-sighted and which I cannot do as I have asthma though I hope next term to play tennis and rounders.

I have not had asthma once since I have been here! I had it all the time in London. Dad says it was pollution and that is why he is in Saudi Arabia, to earn money so we can buy a house of our own in the country. When he first went away I thought a year would never pass but I see now that it will. I also thought that I would hate being at a boarding school and cried my first night here but now I love it and would like to stay only unfortunately I don't think we will be able to afford it as it is only for rich people and even after Saudi Arabia Dad will not be rich.

Anyhow that is enough of me. Please write back when you have time!

With lots of love from
   your sort-of cousin
      Hannah

Chapter Six

"Let's go through the later ones first."

Lucy and Hannah were sitting together in the senior library. Alison Thomas, one of the sixth-formers who had also stayed on, had given them special permission "as it's for serious research". In front of them was a pile of old school magazines dating from the war years.

"You do 1943," said Lucy, "I'll do 1944. Just see if you can see her name anywhere."

"I might as well look for Dorothy too," said Hannah.

"Yes, and my gran. Elizabeth Philpotts. Tell me if you see Elizabeth Philpotts."

Hannah reached for 1943 and opened it at page 1.

"*Editors*," she read, "*Elspeth Dyer and Elizabeth Philpotts*. Hey! I've found her already!"

"Who? My gran? Where?" Lucy peered short-sightedly. She had to hold things about five centimetres in front of her to be able to read them.

"One of the editors," said Hannah. "Oh, and look! Miss Ruskin!"

"Who's Miss Ruskin?"

"She was the one that – that girl was asking about."

"You mean she was here in 1943?"

"Well. . ." Hannah hesitated. 1943 was rather a long time ago. "I suppose it's the same person," she said, suddenly doubtful.

"What's it say about her?"

"It just says, *The editors would like to express their thanks to Miss Ruskin for giving so generously of her time*. It *could* have been her," said Hannah, "'cause when I asked Mrs Dukes she said she thought she'd retired about five years ago. So that would make it about right, wouldn't it?"

Lucy frowned. Her mental arithmetic was rather better than Hannah's.

"It would make her incredibly old."

"Well, some teachers are incredibly old," said Hannah. "Look at Miss Porter."

"Not that old," muttered Lucy. Hannah simply had no idea. She was the sort of person who could add two and two together and make them come to five. Lucy shook her head.

"Games teams," she said, going back to her own magazine. "Here's *your* gran."

"Oh! Where? Let me see!"

"There." Lucy jabbed a finger. "The school won a shield and D. Carter was in the first eleven . . . I don't think my gran was into games. She was more like me: academic. That's why she was an editor. I wouldn't mind being an editor," said Lucy. "When I grow up, I mean. I'd like to work in a publisher's. What do you think you'll do?"

"Dunno." Hannah was back in 1943. Girl Guides, school outings, theatre visits, lower school picnic . . .

"They went on a *picnic*!" said Hannah, entranced. "There's a picture of them. What fun!"

"I don't like picnics," said Lucy. "Wasps get into things and one time I went on one I sat in a cowpat."

"Yeeurgh! Horrible! What happened?"

"I *smelt*," said Lucy. "I had to take my knickers off and wear my cousin's underpants."

Hannah giggled.

"I didn't think it was very funny," said Lucy.

"Well, it probably wasn't at the time," agreed Hannah, "but it's the sort of thing you could *make* funny... You could write about it for the magazine."

Lucy sniffed. She had better things to write about than sitting in cowpats, thank you very much.

"There's a funny poem here," said Hannah. "Listen ...

"They say the camera never lies
What hope is there for me?
With bunny teeth and fishlike eyes
They say the camera never lies
Above it I should try to rise

Since Beauty I can't be.
They say the camera never lies
What hope is there for me?"

"I don't think *that's* very good," said Lucy.

"Why does she keep repeating things? Ran out of ideas, I suppose."

"She wasn't very old."

"How do you know?"

"It says. Georgina Redmayne..." Hannah stopped. Her brow crinkled. "Georgina Redmayne ... Twelve and a half."

"Twelve and a half? I could do better than that," said Lucy. "I should think even you could."

"I thought it was funny," said Hannah.

Lucy didn't have much of a sense of humour. She was the first to admit it. She said that life was too serious to be a laughing matter. Charlotte, on the other hand, said that laughing was all you *could* do. She said you'd die of misery if you didn't have a good laugh. Hannah thought that on the whole she tended to agree with Charlotte.

She worked her way carefully through all

the pages for 1943 but disappointingly found no mention of Margaret.

"Of course," said Lucy, "we don't actually know when she was killed. She might have been dead by 1943."

Hannah shivered.

"What's the matter?" said Lucy. "Are you cold?"

"No. I thought I felt something." Hannah turned to look over her shoulder.

"What sort of something?"

"Something touching me."

"Ghosts from the past. We're probably disturbing them. You have to remember," said Lucy, "that loads of these people will be dead by now."

Hannah did wish that Lucy wouldn't talk so glibly about people being dead! It was all very well when you didn't know them, but when you had read their poems and seen their photographs it brought it home to you that once upon a time they had been real living human beings who had played hockey and gone on picnics and laughed and talked just the same as anyone else. The girl who had written the poem, for instance: Georgina Redmayne. She might even have been in the same form as Margaret. They might have sat and giggled together, making bunny teeth and pulling silly faces.

"Try 1942," said Lucy.

Obediently, Hannah reached out for the next magazine. She found Margaret Carter on page 6. She, too, had written a poem, but hers was not a funny one. It was entitled "My Cousin Kenneth".

My cousin Kenneth is blond and fair,
He flies aeroplanes in the air.
He's going to be an RAF ace
And meet the enemy face to face.
He'll rat-a-tat and shoot them down,
Fighting for Britain and the Crown.
Then he'll get the DFC –
A credit to the family!

She showed it rather shyly to Lucy. She had a feeling that perhaps this really *wasn't* a very good poem. "Blond and fair" – didn't they mean the same thing? And "flying aeroplanes in the air". Where else would you fly an aeroplane?

"She was only eleven," pleaded Hannah.

For once Lucy chose to be kind.

"It's the sort of patriotic stuff they wrote in those days."

"And she was in love with him."

"And that, as well. It doesn't help."

"I'll copy it down," said Hannah. "We can include it in the project."

It was lunchtime when they had finished looking through the magazines. They had found some more mentions of Dorothy, and also of Elizabeth Philpotts, but no more of Margaret.

"You must ask your Cousin Helen *exactly* when she was killed," said Lucy. "We'll need to give the date."

"I've already written to her," said Hannah. "She might send some photographs, as well."

After lunch they looked at school photographs. Modern ones were kept in the main entrance hall, framed and behind glass, but for the older ones they had to ask Mrs Wade, who was Miss Appleyard's secretary.

"I'm not really supposed to be working this week," said Mrs Wade. "I'm supposed to be taking things easy. But if it's really important—"

"It's for our project," said Hannah.

"About the war," added Lucy.

"The war . . . any particular year?"

"We don't really know," said Hannah.

"We could try 1942," said Lucy.

"1942? Wait there; I'll see what I can do."

"We can always come and have another look," said Lucy, "when we know when she died."

"Yes, and when we've got a photograph and know what she looked like."

Mrs Wade returned, waving a scroll.

"Here you are. One school photograph, 1942. You'd better take it to the library – and make sure you bring it back by three o'clock!"

"We will," promised Hannah.

They scampered back to the library with their booty and spread it out on one of the big tables.

"We'll need to put something at each end to keep it flat," said Lucy. "Get some dictionaries!"

The photograph for 1942 showed the entire school, all 350 pupils, standing in four long rows with the staff sitting solemnly in the middle. What struck Hannah immediately was the uniform that the girls were wearing: strange shapeless tunics with square-cut necks and wide box pleats, loosely tied at the waist with sashes.

"You know that girl?" said Hannah slowly.

"Which girl?"

"The one I keep seeing."

"You mean the one I falsely accused." Lucy nodded. "What about her?"

Hannah pointed to the photograph. "That's what she wears."

"It's what my mum used to wear. I've seen pictures."

"Yes, but your mum was *here* – at the school!" How had Daisy come by it?

Lucy shrugged. "It was probably stuff that someone had grown out of. They were probably going to chuck it and one of the domestics took a fancy to it. It could even have been her mum! She probably worked here. And that's why she's got this thing about the place and why she likes dressing up in the uniform. The girl, I mean. Probably makes her think she's one of us. That'll be why she's always mooning around. Obviously a bit loopy."

Since Hannah herself had reluctantly come to the same conclusion, there wasn't very much that she could say. It was true that Daisy *did* moon around. And she certainly seemed obsessed with the school and its occupants.

"I wonder which one is Miss Ruskin?" said Hannah, studying the row of teachers.

"She'd have to be one of the younger ones ... this one?"

"Ugh! No! She's ugly."

Miss Ruskin had been beautiful. Daisy had said so.

"Her!" Hannah stabbed a finger at a slender figure in a neat suit with a brooch on the lapel and a string of what looked like pearls round her neck. Long fair hair reached to her shoulders and wide-apart eyes stared gravely at the camera. "I bet that was her."

"You're just fantasizing," said Lucy. "Shove over! I'm trying to find my gran."

Lucy moved her face along the photograph like a blind worm, nose almost touching the paper. "I *think* that's her. I'm not sure."

"Where? Let me see!"

Lucy pointed to a small, dark-haired, rather sharp-nosed girl standing amongst the ranks of what Hannah supposed must have been prefects, since they all wore badges marked

"Fancy! They still wore uniforms even in the sixth form." Today's sixth wore whatever they liked. "I wish we had uniforms like that."

"*I* don't," said Lucy. "I think they're positively foul."

"Mmm ... the tunic things are a bit weird, I suppose. But I love the sashes!"

"My mum calls them girdles," said Lucy. "They were all different colours, according to which house you were in. My mum's was red, because she was in Stuart. Then there was Windsor and York and Tudor. I wouldn't mind still having houses," said Lucy. "I don't know why they did away with them. Why is your mouth drooping open?"

Hannah closed it, hastily.

"It makes you look half-witted," said Lucy. "You haven't had a seizure or something, have you?"

"No. Tell me about the houses. Which colour sash – I mean girdle – was it for Windsor?"

"I don't know. I only know Stuart."

"Windsor must have been blue," said Hannah.

"Why? Is that the royal colour? I don't know much about royalty," said Lucy. "I'm a republican myself."

"It was blue," said Hannah. She knew that it was because Daisy had told her. *That's Windsor, that is.*

"Are you into royalty?" said Lucy.

Hannah blushed. "Not specially. It's just something I picked up."

"A snippet of information. Off the back of a matchbox, I expect."

Hannah agreed, gratefully, that it probably had been off the back of a matchbox. She felt the less said about Daisy, the better.

Between them, by the end of the day, they

had made three pages of notes and copied out another two pages of bits and pieces from the school magazine.

"But it's not enough," urged Lucy, as they took the precious photograph back to Mrs Wade at three o'clock. "What we really need to do is interview someone who was here at the time. It's a pity my gran isn't still alive or I could have asked her."

"I don't expect anyone's still alive," said Hannah.

Lucy tutted impatiently.

"Of course they are! How long ago do you think it was? Ancient Egypt? It was only this *century*. People can easily live to be eighty-something."

"Mrs Rumbold's grandmother is ninety-three," said Hannah.

"Well, there you are! That proves my point. And anyway, what about this cousin person of yours? She's still alive, isn't she?"

"She didn't come here."

Lucy rolled her eyes. "So we need to find someone who did! I shall ask Mrs Wade," said Lucy.

"Ask me tomorrow," said Mrs Wade, "when I've had a chance to sleep on it."

That evening, on her way back to the common room with two bedtime cups of hot chocolate for herself and Lucy, Hannah was startled by the sudden appearance of a figure slipping out of the shadows just ahead of her.

"You again!" She hissed it angrily. What was Daisy doing here at this time of night? What was she doing here at *all*? Actually daring to come into the school!

"Look what you've made me do," grumbled Hannah. "I've gone and spilt hot chocolate all down myself. I'm sick of being nice to you! You just take advantage. I've told you over and *over*—"

"Please!" whispered Daisy. She clasped her hands beseechingly to her bosom. Not that you could call it a bosom, thought Hannah. It was too scrawny for that.

"Please what?" she said. "Why aren't you indoors?"

Daisy looked puzzled. "I *am* indoors."

"*In your own home.*"

"Please," begged Daisy. "I just want to

hear the end of the story."

"What story?"

"The one you were telling me."

"If you mean about Margaret and Kenneth, I've written to ask my Cousin Helen and I'm still waiting to hear. I *said*," said Hannah, "that I would *tell* you. And I *will*. But not unless you go away and stop bothering me! You'll get us both into trouble. Now you just go away." She pointed sternly up the passage. "Go on! Quickly! Before someone catches you."

Hannah stomped crossly back to the common room. Daisy was getting beyond a joke. She didn't like to admit it, but she was beginning to think that Lucy had been right. She should have gone to Miss Appleyard a long time ago. It was too late now. If she went now, Miss Appleyard would want to know why it had taken her so long. And Hannah wouldn't have any excuse, except to say "I felt sorry for her", and somehow she didn't think Miss Appleyard would accept that. But even Hannah could see that strange girls couldn't be allowed to wander in and out of the school as they felt like it. *Any* girls. Not just one from the estate.

"Heavens!" Lucy took her nose out of her book as Hannah walked back into the common room. "You've gone and spilt hot chocolate all down yourself!"

"I *know*," said Hannah. "Thank you very *much*."

"Oh! Hoity toity!" said Lucy. "Sorry I spoke!"

Next morning, early, they presented themselves at the office.

"Ah, yes!" said Mrs Wade. "The two historians. I've been doing some thinking, and I've come to the conclusion that the best thing you can do is ring the secretary of the Old Girls' Association. Here." She handed Lucy a slip of paper. "That's her number; don't lose it. Her name is Gillian Weir. Mrs Weir. She'll be able to help you if anyone can."

"Who's going to do it?" said Lucy, as they left the office. "You or me?"

"You," said Hannah. She wasn't shy but she felt that Lucy would be better at explaining. Lucy could use adult-sounding language and didn't trip over her words as Hannah sometimes did.

"Right," said Lucy. "Let's go and do it straight away."

Hannah stood at Lucy's side as she made the call. She heard Lucy explain how they were doing research for a project, and then Mrs Weir at the other end said something and Lucy said, "That would be really helpful," and then Mrs Weir said something else and Lucy said *"Really?"* and began to scribble furiously in her project notebook.

"We'll do that," said Lucy, when she had finished scribbling. "Thank you very much indeed."

"Do what? What is it?" said Hannah, trying to read upside down.

"You'll never guess," said Lucy. "She's given me your Miss Ruskin's number!"

"Miss *Ruskin*?"

"She's in a retirement home," said Lucy, "just a bit further up the coast, and what she loves more than anything is visits from old girls."

"But we're not old girls," worried Hannah.

"Doesn't matter. We're at the Hovel. She'll still love to hear from us; Mrs Weir said so. I'm going to telephone her," said Lucy, "and see if I can fix something up."

Hannah listened breathlessly as Lucy dialled the number of Miss Ruskin's retirement home and asked to speak to Miss Ruskin. She heard her explain yet again that they were doing research. Then she heard Lucy say, "Saturday afternoon would be brilliant," and start scribbling all over again.

"There!" Lucy bounced the phone back on to its rest. "You're going to meet your Miss Ruskin at last! She said we can go and interview her at two o'clock on Saturday afternoon. And she's going to give us cakes to eat. She's going to go and buy some from her local shop. It's called Bondolfi's and it does scrummy things like cream horns. She says she always goes there when old girls are coming. Or any girls. She really *loves* talking to people about school."

"I hope she can remember who Margaret was."

"According to Mrs Weir, she remembers everybody. Everybody that was ever a pupil. We," gloated Lucy, "are going to do the best project of anyone!"

My dear Hannah,

It was lovely to hear from you again so soon. I am really enjoying this correspondence! It is giving me a new lease of life. I have told Pan that you will be coming to us for the holidays and he is greatly pleased and purring mightily.

Do by all means bring your friend Lucy; she sounds a most interesting person. I look forward to our having lots of heated debates!

I wonder if it would be a good idea for me to write to your father and formally ask his permission? Maybe you could give me his address and I will do it right away.

Now, to try and answer your questions. I cannot r—

Chapter Seven

" **S**orry, Hannah! No time for reading letters just at the moment. Visit to the dentist, remember?"

Hannah looked up from Cousin Helen's letter to find Miss Archer, the assistant matron, beaming broadly at her as if a visit to the dentist were the greatest fun on earth. Lucy groaned.

"It's not fair, at half term!"

"Specially when everyone else is on holiday."

"Yes, and *last* time," said Lucy, "he stuck this needle in so deep I thought it was going to come out through the top of my head."

Miss Archer laughed, totally unfeeling.

"What a couple of whingeing ninnies! Go and get your coats on. I'll meet you outside."

It was all very well for Miss Archer. She wasn't going to have to sit in the dentist's chair and be subjected to torture.

"It's so foul," grumbled Lucy, as she and Hannah went upstairs to fetch their coats. "It makes your lips go all big and baggy so you can't talk properly."

"What I don't like is the way they whizz about with their drills," said Hannah. "Imagine if their hand slipped or they suddenly went mad – you'd end up without any mouth!"

"Thank you very much," said Lucy. "That's all I need."

"Well, you started it, going on about needles coming out of the top of your head. I s'pose I shall have to read this later." Reluctantly, Hannah put Cousin Helen's letter back in its envelope, peering inside as she did so. "Oh, goody! She's sent me some photos."

"Lots?"

"No. Just a couple."

"Let's see!"

"Not now." Hannah whisked the envelope out of Lucy's reach. "I'll leave it here and we can look when we get back."

"We might not be feeling up to it then! Not if we've got needles sticking out of our heads and half our mouths drilled away."

"I can't help that," said Hannah.

She laid the envelope on her bedside table and placed her library book on top of it. She was reading *Charlotte's Web* for about the nineteenth time. Lucy said that it was babyish – *she* was reading Charles Dickens – but Hannah didn't care. She thought that sometimes you should be allowed to be a bit babyish if you felt like it. It was a great comfort, reading something that you had read before and knew almost off by heart.

"Why don't we take the letter with us and look at it on the way?" demanded Lucy, but Hannah stood firm.

"You can't enjoy things properly with the dentist hanging over you."

"*I* can," boasted Lucy.

"Well, I can't," said Hannah. "And anyway, it's my letter. I'll say when we read it."

The visit to the dentist wasn't as bad as they had feared. No needles came out through their heads, no drills whizzed out of control, no lips went baggy.

"Not a single filling!" gloated Lucy.

"Nor me," said Hannah. "He just poked and prodded a bit."

"Yes, with that wire thing. One day he's going to poke so hard," said Lucy, "it's going to tear a hole in my gum."

As Miss Archer pointed out, he hadn't actually torn a hole in her gum *today*, so that had to be cause for celebration.

"Coffee and cakes," she said. "To help you get over the terrible experience."

The cakes were all squidgy and creamy and just the sort of thing the dentist would probably frown upon, but once in a while, said Miss Archer, it never hurt anyone. What Miss Archer didn't realize, thought Hannah, gleefully helping herself to a particularly glorious and gluggy specimen, was that the very next day they were going to have more cakes with

Miss Ruskin. She hoped that Miss Ruskin's would be squidgy and creamy too!

"Now," said Miss Archer, "what do you want to do? Have a look round town or go straight back?"

Lucy and Hannah exchanged glances.

"Go straight back," they chorused.

Miss Archer seemed surprised. "Is school that attractive?"

Gravely, Lucy said, "We have things to do for our project."

The truth was that neither of them could wait to read Cousin Helen's letter. Back at school they flew up the stairs two at a time, with Lucy as usual tripping over her own feet and Hannah getting out of breath (but not too badly), and tumbled along the passage towards the dorm. As they opened the door Hannah had the strangest feeling that she felt something brush past her. She turned sharply, but the passage was empty. Except – except for the faintest hint of blue disappearing round the corner...

"Come on, come on, come on!" Lucy had torn off her coat and was bouncing impatiently on Hannah's bed. "The suspense is killing me!"

Hannah shook herself. She moved slowly into the dorm and closed the door.

"What is that word," she said, "when you start to see things that aren't really there?"

Lucy went on bouncing. "What are you talking about?"

"When you see things," said Hannah. "What is it called?"

"A mirage? Like in the desert?"

"But what's it called when you *do* it?"

Lucy cackled. "Raving bananas!" she said. She stopped bouncing and sat up. "Do you mean hallucinate?"

Yes, that was exactly what she meant. She was starting to hallucinate. And the dentist hadn't even given her an injection!

"What do you think causes it?" she said.

"Heat stroke? High temperature? Vivid imagination?"

Hannah wasn't suffering from heat stroke and she didn't have a high temperature; at least she didn't think she had. She put a hand to her forehead. No, it felt just the same as it always felt. That only left vivid imagination.

It was true that Mrs Allsopp, marking the last lot of essays they had done, had said that Hannah showed excellent powers of invention. Hannah had been rather puffed up about it at the time. But she wasn't going to be puffed up if it meant seeing Daisy all over the place!

How could she see someone who wasn't there? Unless—

Unless she was seeing a *ghost*?

No! How could Daisy be a ghost? Ghosts didn't talk, ghosts didn't leave feathers in secret posting boxes. It had to be Hannah, hallucinating.

Lucy was growing impatient again.

"Are we going to read this letter or are you going to go on burbling?"

Hannah pulled herself together. "Going to read the letter."

She reached out for it and gave a cry. "Someone's moved it!" She had purposely left it underneath *Charlotte's Web*; now it was on top.

"Not me," said Lucy. "I haven't touched it."

"Well, someone has!"

"I bet it was one of the domestics."

Lucy's first thought was always to blame the domestics; either the domestics or the people who lived on the estate. Sometimes they were one and the same.

"Well, who else could it be?" Lucy stared at Hannah challengingly. Hannah would say that she was being prejudiced, but you had to face facts.

"There isn't anyone else here. Unless you think Miss Appleyard's going to come creeping round reading people's private mail."

No, of course Hannah didn't think that. She wasn't quite sure what she did think. Slowly she took the letter out of its envelope and settled herself on the bed next to Lucy.

"I'll read it out to you, shall I?

"*My dear Hannah,*

It was lovely to hear from you again so soon. I am really enjoying this correspondence! It is giving me a new lease of life. I have told Pan that you will be coming to visit him over the holidays and he is greatly pleased and purring mightily.

Do by all means bring your friend Lucy; she sounds a most interesting person." (Lucy preened.) "I look forward to our having lots of heated debates!

I wonder if it would be a good idea for me to write to your father and formally ask his permission? Maybe you could give me his address and I will do it right away.

Now, to try and answer your questions. I cannot remember the exact date that poor little Megs was killed but it was some time in March or April, 1942. I'm afraid I never really knew the details – I was only fifteen at the time – but I believe it was a direct hit and that she was killed outright. In other words, she did not suffer. But still it was a tragedy, and made all the worse since the school was considered to be in a safe area. They never expected to be bombed, but just occasionally a plane heading for, say, London would get into difficulties and have to turn back, and then they would simply drop the bomb wherever they chanced to be. Poor Megs was just unlucky.

I am sure you do not need me to lecture you on the horrors of war and that doing this project will all too vividly bring it home to you.

I'm afraid I have only managed to unearth a couple of photographs. One is of my brother Kenneth in his RAF uniform, the other of the three of us, Dotty, Megs and me, on holiday in Weston-super-Mare in August 1936. Dotty was then about ten or eleven, I was nine, and Megs six. Unfortunately it is not very good of Megs. She is a bit blurred, but there are lots more hidden away in a box somewhere down in the cellar, so perhaps when you and Lucy come you can have fun searching for them. In the meantime, these two are for you to keep if you would like them.

About Kenneth. Very sadly, he was lost in a bombing raid only a few months after Megs was killed. I fear that by now you will be starting to think the story is nothing but doom and gloom, but indeed that is what war is all about." ("*Right.*" Lucy nodded vigorously.)

"*Now, turning to happier matters, let me say how pleased I am that you are enjoying yourself at 'the Hovel'. Your mother would have been thrilled. She always wanted you to go there because she loved it so much herself. Mind you, she was homesick to begin with! I remember her once telling me, years later when we were both grown up, how she had cried herself to sleep every night for a week. She said it wasn't until one of the other girls in her dormitory heard her and crept out of bed to comfort her that she began to feel a bit more cheerful and decided that perhaps boarding school wasn't so bad after all."*

Hannah broke off. "Isn't that extraordinary?"

"What?" said Lucy.

"Well ... *that*," said Hannah, "happening to my mum!"

"I suppose it is a bit unusual," agreed Lucy. "Mostly people cry quietly so they can't be heard. In case anyone laughs at them, you know. Not that anyone would. At least, I wouldn't. Though I might think it a bit wimpish. *I* never cried. Did you?"

"M-me?" Hannah was taken aback. So it hadn't been Lucy who had comforted her! It must have been Charlotte or Danny, after all. "Only just a very little bit," she said.

"I never heard you." Lucy tapped at the letter. "Go on! What else does she say?"

"Um ... *wasn't so bad after all. Strangely enough she never discovered who it was that had taken pity on her. She used to mention it quite often. It was one of the great unsolved mysteries of her schooldays.*

If you are happy where you are and would like to stay there, I am sure that could be arranged. Would you allow me to pay for you?" (Hannah gasped.) "*As you know, I have no children of my own, nor any nephews or nieces. In fact, my cousin–sort–of, you are my closest living relative! I would regard it as a privilege to be allowed to help. Your mother would be overjoyed to think of you being at her old school and I would very much like to do this in her memory, if your father would agree. May I mention it when I write to him? You must let me know.*"

"Wow!" said Lucy.

Hannah was covered in confusion.

"I hope she doesn't think I only got in touch 'cause I wanted something from her."

"Well, but you did," pointed out Lucy. "You wanted to know more about your grandmother."

"I didn't want *money*."

"But you won't say no?" Lucy sounded suddenly anxious. "If she really wants to pay for you?"

"I suppose it's up to Dad," said Hannah.

"Tell her to write to him! Give her his address! Just think," urged Lucy. "We could be together all the way up the school!"

"I'll write straight away," promised Hannah.

"Does she say anything else?"

"No, just love. Let's look at the pictures."

Hannah tipped up the envelope. A photograph fell out. It showed the three girls, Dorothy, Helen and Margaret, paddling in the sea. The two older girls were wearing bathing caps, so that you couldn't see their hair. The bigger one, who had to be Dorothy, was what Hannah's dad would have called "strapping". No wonder she had played hockey, thought Hannah. The one that was Helen was thinner and prettier. Hannah liked the look of her. But of course it was Margaret she was most interested in.

"Let's see!" Lucy craned over, peering short-sightedly. "Which one's your gran?"

"That one." Hannah pointed. Lucy moved in closer.

"Goodness! You don't look in the *least* bit like her. She looks quite disagreeable. Which is Margaret? The littlest one?"

It must have been a chilly day when the photograph was taken. Margaret was standing with her hands held up like bunny paws, her cheeks sucked in. She had obviously been shivering, which was perhaps why the photograph was a bit fuzzy. Unlike the other two she wasn't wearing a bathing cap, so that you could see her hair was blonde, done up in a complicated arrangement of plaits on top of her head.

"She looks like you," announced Lucy.

"Do you think so?" Hannah snatched the photograph back. She frowned as she considered it. "How can you tell?"

"She's got the same nose."

"Mmm..." Perhaps there was a faint

resemblance, but only very faint. "She's plump," said Hannah.

"I was talking about her face."

"That's plump too."

"Chubby," said Lucy. "I expect she'd have grown out of it. I used to be chubby when I was that age."

Hannah studied the photograph with a growing sense of wonderment.

"She'd have been my mum's aunt!"

"That's why she looks like you. Let's see gorgeous Kenneth."

Hannah held the envelope upside down and shook it.

"Where's it gone?" She opened the envelope and looked inside it. "Where is it? It was here before! I saw it!"

"It must have fallen out."

They crawled round the dormitory on hands and knees, searching under beds and picking up the corners of rugs. The photograph was nowhere to be found.

"Oh!" wailed Hannah. "And I wanted to know what he was like!"

"Are you sure it was there?"

"Yes! Positive!" She had peeped into the envelope when she had had to put the letter back that morning. She had had just one tantalizing glimpse of a dark-haired young man in RAF uniform.

"*She* must have taken it!"

Hannah looked at Lucy, startled.

"Whoever it was," said Lucy, "that read the letter. They obviously saw the photograph and took a fancy to it. Slipped it in their pocket, I bet," said Lucy.

Hannah was silent.

"We ought to report it. People can't go round just helping themselves to other people's photographs. I bet it was that Glenys! The one with the squinty eyes. She's got all these photographs of film stars. She told me," said Lucy. "She's got them all over her bedroom wall. I bet she took Kenneth to add to her collection."

"Why would she do that?" said Hannah. "Kenneth wasn't a film star."

"No, but he was handsome. Your Helen person said so. Let's go and find someone and tell them about it!"

"I can't be bothered," said Hannah. "It's only a photograph. There's bound to be more, when we go in the holidays."

"But it's stealing!"

Yes, thought Hannah, and I know who stole it. Not poor Glenys with her squinty eyes but that wretched Daisy. Hannah hadn't been whatever-the-word was – seeing mirages. It really had been Daisy. *Daring*, for a second time, to come into school! To come all the way upstairs to the dormitory! It meant that Lucy had been right all along: Daisy was a thief. Stealing someone's photograph was every bit as bad as stealing their money. And if she thinks she can give me another measly old feather in exchange, thought Hannah, I'll—

Hannah was so cross she couldn't think what she would do.

"Let's go down and eat," she said. "I'm starving."

Lucy couldn't say anything over lunch because Miss Archer came into the dining hall and sat with them and they had to make polite conversation, but as soon as they were on their own again she started.

"You oughtn't to let people get away with that sort of thing! And what are you going to tell to your Helen person? After all the trouble she's been to – *finding* it for you, *giving* it to you. . ."

Nag, nag, nag! thought Hannah.

"I'll go and do her a letter right away," she said. Anything to stop Lucy going on at her. "I'll see you later."

Lucy, fortunately, had to go and have a serious talk with Miss Appleyard about confirmation classes. Lucy had recently decided that she didn't believe in God any more and therefore how could she be confirmed? She was going to tell this to Miss Appleyard. Hannah thought it rather bold, but then Lucy was like that. Hannah wouldn't have dared.

They parted company, Lucy going off to Miss Appleyard's study, Hannah to the junior common room. It was strange being in there by herself, without any of the others. By Sunday evening they would all be back and Lucy would be complaining again about the lack of privacy.

Hannah took her writing pad out of her locker. Before writing to Cousin Helen there was something else she had to do. Choosing her blackest and thickest magic marker, and using big, cross capital letters, she wrote:

I KNOW THAT IT WAS YOU WHO TOOK MY PHOTOGRAPH OF KENNETH. KINDLY GIVE IT BACK TO ME *IMMEDIATELY*. OTHERWISE I SHALL REPORT YOU.

She took it out to the letter box and angrily thrust it into the hole.

"Daisy," she said, "if you're listening, *I really mean this!*"

Lucy returned as Hannah was writing her letter to Cousin Helen.

"What happened?" said Hannah.

"Oh, we had a little talk and Miss Appleyard said that she quite understood. She said," said Lucy, "that it was better to bring these things out into the open than be a hypocrite and live a lie."

"So aren't you going to be confirmed?"

"No," said Lucy. "Are you telling Cousin Helen about the photograph?"

Hannah made a mumbling sound, which could have been taken as "yes" or might simply have been a frog in her throat. She had decided that she wouldn't break the news to Cousin Helen just yet. She would give Daisy one last chance.

She finished her letter, sealed it up quickly before Lucy could demand to know what she had said, and went off to post it in the box at the end of the drive. On her way back, without very much hope but just as she happened to be passing, she stuck her hand into the hole in the wall. To her amazement, the photograph was there. Daisy had returned her photograph! Handsome Kenneth, in all the glory of his RAF uniform. She could see why Daisy had been tempted: he had been *very* good-looking.

Hannah scuttled triumphantly back into school, clutching her photograph.

"Look!" She burst in upon Lucy, nose-in-a-book as usual. "I found it!"

"Where?"

"In my pocket." Hannah crossed her fingers behind her back as she said it. "I must have taken it out this morning without realizing."

"*Honestly!*" said Lucy. "You're getting so vague it's just not true!"

Dear Dad,

I hope you are well. I am well. I still have not had asthma. I think you were right and it was the pollution so please next term can I play games?

You know you said write to Helen Banfield and I did and she wrote back and said to call her Cousin Helen which I told you on the telephone? Dad she has asked me if I would like to go and stay with her in the holidays and I can take Lucy as well as she is my best friend, so can I Dad? I have given her your address in Saudi Arabia and she is going to write to you about it.

Something else she is going to write to you about and that is school. She has said she will pay for me if I want to stay here after you come back!!! Dad CAN I? I would miss not seeing you in term time but maybe if we could buy a house near to the school I could come home at weekends which is what some of the girls do. Please say I can! I have got used to being here and I don't think it would be good for me to have to start again somewhere else.

It has just been half term and I have been to the dentist!!! But I didn't have to have any fillings so that was all right.

I am still counting the days but sometimes what I do now is wait until a whole week has passed and then cross it off. It is easier to count weeks than days.

I must stop now as it is nearly time for bed. We are allowed to stay up quite late while it is half term although Lucy would like to stay up even later. She would like to stay up until midnight, just reading! What she does is read under the bedclothes. She has a big torch which she bought specially. I tell her she will ruin her eyes but she says this is nonsense. Lucy reads EVERY-WHERE. Even on buses. This is how she knows so much.

Lots and lots of love and kisses
from

Hannah x

Chapter Eight

Sitting on the bus on the way to Miss Ruskin's, Hannah suddenly discovered that she felt nervous. She couldn't imagine why; she didn't usually feel shy about meeting people. She turned, rather urgently, to Lucy.

"Couldn't we just have talked to her on the phone?"

"What?" Lucy looked at her in surprise.

"On the telephone," said Hannah. "You could have interviewed her on the telephone!"

"She *invited* us," said Lucy.

"Yes, I know. But—"

"She likes having visitors. She doesn't get that many. And anyway, she's buying cakes."

Hannah subsided. She sat with her cheek pressed against the window, feeling the vibrations of the bus.

"What's the problem?" said Lucy.

Hannah humped a shoulder. She wasn't really sure, though she thought perhaps it might have something to do with the passing of time. Miss Ruskin in the photograph – if it *had* been Miss Ruskin in the photograph – had been young and pretty. Miss Ruskin in her retirement home was going to be old and wrinkled. Did Hannah really want to see her like that? When once she had been so beautiful?

"It's all right," said Lucy kindly. "I'll do the talking. Just leave it to me."

Miss Ruskin's retirement home was a large old house on the sea front. Hannah, who had once heard Mrs Rumbold telling Dad about the home that her grandmother was in ("Disgusting! Stinks of cabbage and you-know-what. And rows of old folk just sitting about like mummies."), was rather scared that Seacrest House might be the same. She watched as Lucy confidently pressed one of the bells by the side of the door. After a few seconds an intercom crackled into life.

"Hallo? Is that Hannah and Lucy?"

Lucy put her mouth close to the speaker. "Yes," she said. "It's us."

"Good girls! You're on time. I like people to be punctual."

There was a click, and Lucy pushed at the door and stepped boldly inside. Hannah crept after her, fearful of what she might find. She needn't have worried. There was no stink of cabbage or you-know-what, no rows of old folk sitting like mummies. Seacrest House smelt of wood and furniture polish. A large vase of flowers stood on a table. And not an old person was in sight!

A tall figure was coming down the stairs towards them.

"Hannah! Lucy! Which is which?"

"I'm Lucy," said Lucy. "This is Hannah."

"How kind of you to come! When one gets old, you know, it is a great joy to have visitors."

Miss Ruskin turned and led the way back up the stairs. Lucy and Hannah followed.

Hannah was starting to feel a bit better. It was true that Miss Ruskin was old – even *very* old. Her hair was pure white and she walked with a stick, but still you could tell that she had once been the beautiful Miss Ruskin who wore a pink suit and smelt of flowers. And she *was* the person in the photograph! Hannah had identified her quite correctly.

"Let us be civilized and take tea first," said Miss Ruskin. "After that we can get down to serious business. I always feel," she said, "that one needs sustenance."

Hannah wasn't certain what sustenance meant, but from the way Lucy said, "Oh. Right. Absolutely!" and eyed a plateful of cakes on the top shelf of a tea trolley, she supposed it had to be food.

Miss Ruskin's cakes were every bit as gooey and squidgy as Hannah had hoped.

"Do you like sickly things?" said Miss Ruskin. "Sadly I've grown out of them myself, but I can still remember what it was like to be young. Please eat as many as you can manage; they will only go to waste otherwise."

When all the cakes had been eaten and the

tea had been drunk, Miss Ruskin pushed the trolley to one side and said, "Now! Tell me about this project and how I can be of help."

It was Lucy who did the explaining.

"We've been given this assignment on what it was like at the H— I mean at Madeley Hall in the war. So Hannah decided to try and find out more about her grandmother, 'cause she was there at the time, which mine was as well as a matter of fact, only—"

Miss Ruskin leaned forward. "What were their names?"

"Mine was Elizabeth Philpotts and Hannah's was Dorothy Carter."

"I remember them well! Elizabeth went to Oxford. Dorothy married a barrister. Continue."

"Well, they're both dead now – "

Miss Ruskin nodded. "I saw it in the newsletter."

" – only Hannah never met hers on account of she didn't like Hannah's mum marrying her dad, and so that's why she specially wanted to find out more about her. So she wrote to this cousin—"

"My gran's cousin," said Hannah.

"Her gran's cousin, and she got this letter back saying did Hannah know that her gran had had a sister and that the sister had been killed by a bomb, and that it was the only bomb that ever fell on the school and the sister was the only person to be killed and it just seemed so *poignant*," said Lucy, who obviously enjoyed the word, "that we wanted to base our project on her. And we thought perhaps you might be able to tell us a bit more such as what she was like and how it happened and – and where, and that sort of thing. If you remember her, that is," said Lucy.

"I never forget any of my pupils," said Miss Ruskin. "They are all indelibly engraven on my mind. Poor little Daisy in particular . . . she holds a very special place in my affections."

"Excuse me, did you say . . . *Daisy*?" burst out Hannah.

"Daisy," said Miss Ruskin.

Hannah and Lucy exchanged glances. Lucy was thinking, "She's too old. She's confused." Hannah was thinking something quite different. Her cheeks fired up. She hadn't meant to be rude. But ... *Daisy?*

"We thought her name was Margaret," said Lucy.

"She was always known as Daisy at school. It's a pet name for Margaret. It comes from the French *marguerite*, which is another name for a daisy. It suited her. She was a dear child! Sweet-natured, generous, trusting ... she had a truly sunny personality. With us such a short time, but in that short time she made her mark. Not brilliant academically, but bright as a button for all that. I remember – " a reminiscent smile lit up Miss Ruskin's face – "I remember a poem she wrote for the school magazine. *My cousin Kenneth is blond and fair, He flies aeroplanes in the air...*"

"We saw that one," said Lucy.

Miss Ruskin shook her head. "Appalling verse! But it came from the heart."

"Do you..." Hannah started, and then stopped, not sure whether she really wanted to know the answer to her question.

"Do I?" prompted Miss Ruskin.

Hannah swallowed. "Do you remember a

girl called Anne Marley?"

"Oh, very well!" Miss Ruskin chuckled. "Quite an Amazon! Captain of hockey, captain of netball, captain of cricket ... she was greatly admired by all the younger ones. And rightly so. Under her leadership we won the Southern Schools Shield for both 1942 and '43. No small achievement."

Hannah's thoughts whirled and whizzed inside her head. What could it mean? Daisy, Anne Marley ... it didn't make any sense!

Lucy, meanwhile, in businesslike fashion, had pulled out her pen. The name Anne Marley obviously meant nothing to her. Even Lucy with her great brain was capable of forgetting things from time to time.

"Is it all right," she said, "if I make notes?"

"By all means! That is what you are here for."

"Can you tell us exactly when she died? Margaret, that is."

Miss Ruskin answered promptly: "12th April, 1942. She had the misfortune to be in the sick bay at the time. Nothing much, a touch of earache and sore throat, but Matron felt she needed peace and quiet."

Lucy scribbled furiously.

"She was on her own in there. I think she could never have known what hit her. The sick bay," continued Miss Ruskin, "was demolished. It stood where the new junior science block stands today. I myself," she said, "was on the English staff."

"Was Margaret any good at English?"

"She was ... enthusiastic," said Miss Ruskin. "Let us put it that way. She loved to read – but oh, dear! That everlasting Enid Blyton! She would have grown out of it, no doubt."

Miss Ruskin nodded slowly to herself. Hannah had the feeling that she was slipping back into the past.

"I always wanted to try her on *Jane Eyre*. But she wasn't ready for it. Not quite. She would have come to it. And then all that wealth of English literature! But it was not to be. Fate had other plans."

There was a silence. Hannah didn't like to break it by asking more questions, and perhaps Lucy didn't either, for she had suspended her scribbling.

"She came to me once, you know. Not long after it had happened. Poor little soul! She was so confused. She couldn't seem to grasp the fact that she – she wasn't here any more. She was still hanging on, still clinging, desperately, to the idea of life. I tried my best to explain. I told her, death is just like stepping into the next room. Wait, and they'll all come to you. All those whom you love. Just wait, that is all you have to do. But I fear it meant nothing to her. She couldn't believe, you see, that she was not still with us. That she had passed beyond. She kept saying, *I'm lonely! I'm so lonely!*"

Miss Ruskin's voice sank to a whisper, the whisper of a child.

"It was her cousin she wanted. Her cousin Kenneth. Oh, he was a fine young man! Honest, upright and handsome with it! He was like a beloved older brother to my little Daisy. He had been going to visit her, as I recall. She had been so excited, so looking forward to it! She couldn't understand why he hadn't come. *Where is he?* she kept saying.

Why isn't he here? How could I tell her –"
Miss Ruskin spread her hands – "How could I
tell her that she was the one who was no
longer here?"

The silence fell upon them again. Lucy was
fiddling awkwardly with her pen top. Hannah's cheeks were aglow with the burning
desire to speak – if only she could think of
what she wanted to say. If only Lucy were not
here!

"Somewhere," said Miss Ruskin, "I have a
photograph."

With the aid of her stick she hobbled across
the room and began to rummage in a box that
looked to Hannah to be full of old documents
and newspaper cuttings.

"I have it!" Triumphantly, Miss Ruskin
returned to her seat. She was holding a scroll,
which she handed to Hannah. "Somewhere in
the front row . . . sitting cross-legged with her
hair in plaits."

"1942," said Lucy, peering over Hannah's
shoulder. "That's the one we looked at."

"It was taken the week before she died."

"Oh, that is *really* poignant," said Lucy.

"Which one is she?"

There was a whole long row of little girls sitting cross-legged with their hair in plaits, but Hannah knew at once which one was Daisy. She handed the photograph to Lucy.

"That one."

"Oh, yes!" Lucy screwed her eyes up. "I can see it now ... and she *has* got your nose. And you see, she did stop being chubby!"

"I wish I could think," said Miss Ruskin, "that the poor mite had found peace, but somehow I doubt it. She only came to me the once, but every now and again I used to catch glimpses of her, wandering the school like a little lost soul. I almost felt, on the day I retired, that I was deserting her. Poor child! If she lingers still, she will be amongst strangers. Not a soul who knew her."

"You mean," said Lucy baldly, "that she's a ghost?"

"Her spirit is wandering; she is not at rest. Yet the door to the next room lies open! She has only to step through it."

"So why doesn't she?"

Lucy didn't listen, thought Hannah. Poor

Daisy had never properly grasped the fact that she was dead.

"For some," said Miss Ruskin, "the passing is easy. For others there is much turmoil."

Lucy frowned slightly and looked down at her note pad.

"She needs someone to show her the way. I tried, but alas –" Miss Ruskin leaned forward to take back her photograph – "I failed."

"Do you think," said Hannah, finding her tongue at last, "if she knew about Kenneth—"

"He was killed," explained Lucy, in case Miss Ruskin might not have heard.

"In the war," said Hannah. "I just wondered, if she knew that he was already there, waiting for her ... whether it might help?"

Lucy stared, but Miss Ruskin took the suggestion seriously.

"You mean, help her find peace? If she could only be assured that she would find him there ... I have no doubt that she would go to him. And gladly. But who is there," said Miss Ruskin, "who could tell her?"

On the way back to school on the bus Lucy said, "Why did you ask that about Kenneth?"

"I just thought – maybe – if she knew she wasn't going to be alone..."

Hannah's voice trailed off helplessly.

"You surely didn't *believe* all that about her coming back?"

"Why not?" Hannah jutted her chin. Lucy might be clever, but she didn't know everything.

"Well, honestly!" said Lucy. "It's all make-believe."

"You think Miss Ruskin was just imagining it?"

"She's old," said Lucy. "She's wandering in her mind."

And I'm young and wandering in mine, thought Hannah. She turned to look out of the window. After a few minutes Lucy said, "Are you sulking?"

"No, but I don't think you ought to accuse people of wandering just because they're old."

"But people do wander when they're old! I expect even I will."

"She remembered all her pupils," said

Hannah. She turned back to look at Lucy. "She remembered Anne Marley."

Lucy shunted her spectacles. "Where did you get that name from? It rings a bell ... I suppose we must have seen it in one of the magazines."

Hannah didn't contradict her.

Immediately after tea, Hannah took out her pen and her writing pad. She knew now what she had to do.

Dear Daisy, she wrote, and this time she used proper joined-up writing because Daisy could obviously read perfectly well. She wasn't simple at all, only sad and confused and lonely.

I am sorry I was cross with you and told you to go away. I have been to see Miss Ruskin and she has explained things to me. She told me that you hold a very special place in her affections. She is an old lady now but still beautiful.

Did you read my letter from Cousin Helen? I don't mind if you did. But in case you didn't I will tell you that Kenneth is waiting for you "in the next room" and I think you should go to him as he has been waiting there for a very long time.

I hope you can be at peace now.
With love from
Your friend Hannah x

"Where are you going?" said Lucy, as Hannah folded her sheet of paper.

"Just out," said Hannah. "I won't be a minute."

She couldn't be bothered making things up or inventing excuses any more. She placed the note carefully in the hole-in-the-wall letter box beneath the laurels.

"Goodbye, Daisy," she whispered. "Be happy!"

Later that evening, up in the dorm, Lucy said, "I've just remembered where I heard that name before ... Anne Marley. That was the one that girl asked you about."

"Mmm," said Hannah, jumping into bed.

"But she was here in the war!"

"Mmm," said Hannah.

"So how did she know about her?"

"Dunno," said Hannah.

"I bet her mother told her." Lucy settled herself cosily under the duvet and picked up her book. "The one that was a domestic and got given the uniform. She probably had a thing about her. I bet that's what it was."

"Probably," said Hannah.

Next day was Sunday and they were accompanied to church – just Lucy and Hannah and the three sixth-formers – by Miss Appleyard herself. Lucy explained earnestly to Hannah that although she was now an atheist and didn't believe in God, she had no objection to going to church if that was what Miss Appleyard wanted.

What she really meant was that she had suggested to Miss Appleyard that perhaps she might be allowed to stay behind and read her book, and Miss Appleyard had said, "Don't be silly, Lucy! You know perfectly well that in order not to attend church you need a note from your mother."

"Anyway," said Lucy, "it's company for you. And I don't actually pray; I just sit with my own thoughts."

"That's all right then," said Hannah.

Lucy looked at her rather sharply. She

sometimes suspected that Hannah might secretly be laughing at her.

Coming back from church they walked down the lane by the side of the junior science block. Miss Appleyard and the three sixth-formers were in front, Lucy and Hannah dawdling behind. Nobody except Lucy saw Hannah suddenly dart across the lane and for no apparent reason stick her hand into a hole in the wall.

"What *are* you doing?" said Lucy.

The note had gone. Coiled neatly in its place was Daisy's blue sash that Hannah had admired so much. She pulled it out, blinking hard to keep away the tears.

"What's that?" said Lucy.

"I think it's a present," said Hannah.

"A present? A mouldy old girdle?"

It wasn't a mouldy old girdle. It was Daisy's way of saying thank you. Of saying goodbye.

"Are you crying?" said Lucy.

"No!" Hannah dashed the tears away. Why should she be crying? Daisy had found peace.

"You look as if you are," said Lucy.

"Well, I'm not," said Hannah. "I ought to know!"